Mys.

5

Daughters of Summer

OTHER TITLES IN THE LORD GODWIN SERIES:

Murder on Good Friday

DAUGHTERS
of SUMMER

A LORD GODWIN NOVEL

Sara Conway

CUMBERLAND HOUSE
Nashville, Tennessee

Published by
  Cumberland House Publishing, Inc.
  431 Harding Industrial Drive
  Nashville, TN 37211

Cover design: Unlikely Suburban Design
Text design: Lisa Taylor

Library of Congress Cataloging-in-Publication Data

Conway, Sara, 1962–
    Daughters of summer / Sara Conway.
        p. cm.
    ISBN 1-58182-340-1 (hardcover)
    1. Great Britain—History—Henry III, 1216–1272—Fiction. I. Title.
    PS3603.O68D38 2003
    813'.6—dc21

                                                              2002155046

Printed in the United States of America
1 2 3 4 5 6 7 8 — 08 07 06 05 04 03

This book is dedicated to
Daniel Michael Davis.

Map of Hexham

River Tyne

The Haugh

1. The Priory Cathedral of St. Andrew
2. The Moot Hall
3. Market Square
4. The Keep

N

R. Conway

DAUGHTERS OF SUMMER

⊙ΠE✝

Northumbria, England
1221

They say in the north that spring is like Eve, wanton and defiant—a temptress. She seduces with fleeting thaws and warm breezes, holding out the hope of first fruits, before snatching it away and handing the year back to winter.

But summer is the season of Mary, temperate and serene, everyone's favorite. In this year, however, she grew restless, angry even, and the time of the Virgin quickly changed from mild to hot. May Day was too warm, Midsummer blistering. Fields grew parched and crops began to wither. Folk knew a meager autumn harvest would surely follow and pondered anxiously the long hungry months of winter.

Yet Mary is the mother of mercy, and true to her nature she suddenly withdrew the punishing heat, and with the coming of the feast of St. Olaf, gentler days returned. The folk of Hexham heaved a happy sigh, for not only was their harvest assured, but so also was the success of the shire's annual fair, which begins on the sixth day of every August; fine weather, as everyone knows, draws people to market like moths to a taper.

Now, two days before the fair's opening, local merchants and craftsmen busily mingled alongside those from abroad to cart their wares and tools to the fair site, to the temporary stalls erected on Hexham's haugh, a wide, flat stretch along the River Tyne. These they rented from the owner of the fair and overlord of Hexham, the Archbishop of York, Walter de Gray.

Not that many locals had ever met their lord. A "foreigner," he rarely traveled north from his princely household in York. Folk would scarcely recognize the man they owed duties and obligations, save perhaps by his haughty manner and sumptuous dress, for the archbishop's penchant for regalia was legendary.

His chief vassal in the north was Lord Godwin, Bailiff of Hexhamshire. A capable man, he was prone to lead and encourage, but intolerant of fuss and ceremony. Walking along cobbled Gilesgate, smooth from constant wear, Godwin pondered the ways of his lord, wondering why the archbishop seemed less inclined these days to send his courtly minions north to scrutinize his bailiff's methods. Was he finally satisfied, after two years of service, that Godwin could be trusted to competently carry out his duties of keeping order and dispensing justice?

He was making his way to the fair site, descending from the natural terrace upon which Hexham is situated, traveling in the crowded company of laden-down carts and wagons. He recognized most, but not all, of their drivers. There were shouts of greeting as the bailiff passed by, and when he was well out of hearing, outsiders made inquiries as to his identity.

"Why that's our bailiff, Lord Godwin," a smith from a nearby village answered. He was leading a sturdy pony pulling a cartload of coal. "The nephew of Patric, Earl of Dunbar and Lothian," he added, relishing the effect.

"Earl Patric," they murmured, staring after Godwin's retreating figure.

"He looks like a huntsman, no noble banty cock swaggerin' about!" someone said, dubiously scrutinizing the bailiff's simple attire, his leather tunic and breeches, his well-worn boots and purposeful stride.

"Aye, he's tough as leather and as good natured as a pump," the smith agreed. "He puts on no airs, that one, but don't let looks deceive you!"

Godwin continued along Gilesgate until he had a clear view of the fair. Dodging carts and wagons, he crossed the road to stop and gaze upon the lively industry below. Gilesgate leads directly to the bridge, well built of oaken planks and vigilantly maintained by the shirefolk. This was a service they owed the archbishop, but folk tended the bridge because it was their primary link to kin in the north, to the Marches and Scotland beyond.

Hexham's bridge was also the fairground's official western boundary, marked by a tollbooth. The grounds ran easterly along the haugh, a marshy place in winter when the river runs high, but firm and dry in summer and blanketed by sweet grasses. Another tollbooth, a furlong or so from the first, marked the farthest extent of the fair.

He was pleased to see the stalls standing in orderly rows, properly segregated by trade. Butchers and tanners were grouped close to the river. Next came the booths of craftsmen offering on-the-spot services—metal workers, goldsmiths and ironsmiths. Stalls offering fresh fruits and vegetables, breads, and spices were clustered along the street running parallel to the haugh on Haugh Lane. Nearest to the bridge were the drapers and woolmongers.

His eyes strayed next to the great tent erected at the center of the fair site, built to accommodate the justices from York. They would hear all fair-related pleas, aside from those dealing with serious crime, Godwin's exclusive domain.

Yes, he thought, giving the grounds a final sweeping glance, preparations for the annual event had gone smoothly. Merchants and buyers had been arriving for days and Hexham's accommodations were bursting. Late arrivals would spill into nearby fields to put up tents and make temporary camps. The fair promised to be a successful one.

Unlike his first, he recalled. Then, he had been the new bailiff, just back from crusade. The fair had been a disaster. Godwin had hired local men to serve as watchmen, for his knightly retinue was deserving of rest after the fierce campaigning in the East, followed by the long journey home. This proved to be a grave error, for the lot he chose was negligent. On the first night of their watch, after the curfew, a wandering company of harlots lured them from the fairgrounds. Whilst they were occupied, robbers, in league with the prostitutes it was later proved, came and stole some costly livestock—palfreys and warhorses. They then turned the cattle loose to rampage over the fair site: booths were overturned, merchandise trampled, food spoiled. Reparations had been expensive, borne by the archbishop, who furiously counted the whole event a loss, even when taking into account his profits from stallage tolls.

The only bright note in the debacle had been finding the thieves. Godwin and his knights had hunted them down, capturing them on the Marches. The horses had already been sold, but a hefty sack of silver swung from the belt of the ringleader, and Godwin confiscated this for the archbishop, who was only grudgingly mollified.

He shook his head at the memory, smiling at his greenness. No, it had not been a promising start to a new appointment. He had fully expected the archbishop to renounce their bond of fealty, to find another, more experienced bailiff, despite Godwin's kinship ties; for it was his uncle, Earl Patric, who had intervened to secure the position for his nephew. But the archbishop had taken no action and Godwin, though he did not need the post, yet wanted it, had been grateful.

There was no need to continue to the fair site. All looked well and he had duties waiting in the Moot Hall. He was about to turn back when he caught sight of Asheferth, one of his household knights, signaling to him from the bridge below and wearing a customary scowl. Godwin heaved a sigh. Asheferth was proving to be a difficult knight to instruct. Brooding and willful, he was golden haired with fiercely burning eyes. Women found him pleasing, winning the knight both hearts and envy.

"My lord," he said, coming to an abrupt halt before Godwin, his mail hauberk ringing. "I cannot do as you ask! It is contemptible—" He broke off as the twin daughters of Lord Acomb passed by, trailing a bored groom. They smiled shyly, eyes lowered, and Asheferth quickly executed a bow, as deep as his hauberk would allow. Godwin nodded his greeting, suppressing a smile when he turned back to face his knight. Asheferth adhered strictly to courtly manners and he would not appreciate amusement. "I cannot command ruffians!" he blurted when the ladies were well beyond hearing. "They are villains, unsuitable—"

"Calm yourself, Asheferth. Why must every matter be a drama? Surely, in all the shire you can find eight or so doughty men to serve you. They will not stand guard after curfew, only help patrol the roads and streets, keep their ears cocked for trouble. With hardly an effort, I can think of ten worthy men."

The knight sagged, his outrage suddenly spent. Godwin was growing accustomed to these abrupt changes in temperament, but still they troubled him, and not for the first time in the last several weeks, he wondered what ailed his man.

"It is this business of the fair, my lord," Asheferth complained. "I did not train to deal in such matters. Tolls! Curfews! Tinkers! What have these to do with knighthood? They are beneath us! I do not know how you endure it, lord. You, a crusader and nephew of Earl—"

"Do not meddle in matters you know nothing of, Asheferth," Godwin warned. "My reasons are my own, nor would I offer an account to you."

The knight recoiled, and Godwin, regretting his sharpness, added more kindly, "Knights have other duties besides battle. Keeping justice and protecting folk are worthy services."

"Aye, my lord," he said, eyes on the ground.

Godwin heaved another sigh. "If this business is so burdensome, why did you not go tourneying with the others? It was not I who commanded you to stay, but your own will."

"Aye, and my will is not my own it seems. . . ." He kept his eyes sullenly on the cobbled street.

Godwin frowned. "Explain this riddle, Asheferth. Who commands you to stay in Hexhamshire, if not you or I?"

"Nay, I spoke carelessly, my lord," he said, looking up to meet Godwin's gaze. "Pay no attention to my ramblings." He laughed softly, shaking his fair head.

Godwin continued to eye him. "Is something troubling you, Asheferth?" Godwin knew he wasn't likely to discuss it, but he asked anyway. Nor was his knight likely to confide with any other in the retinue. Though Asheferth had joined Godwin's company some three months ago and was a respectful and attentive novice, he tended to remain aloof from boon companionship.

"Nay, it's nothing, lord," he said. "I'll see to rounding up the men."

"Hold up, Asheferth," Godwin said as the knight was turning away. "You've served me well and a respite is in order, I think. Take a few days to do what you will. I'll see to the extra men myself."

Asheferth brightened instantly. "My thanks, lord!"

"What will you do then? Go tourneying?"

"Nay, hunting!" Then he bounded past Godwin, who turned to watch his knight as he went off in the direction of the stable, as if he would set out that very moment, without gear or provisions. Shaking his head, he thought it must be youth that made Asheferth so erratic. He was but twenty, sixteen years Godwin's junior. Once, he had been as flighty, as restless. . . .

"Lord Godwin!" a voice called, and he turned to see Gruffydd, merchant and local worthy, huffing toward him.

"At last, I've found you!" the man panted as he drew up, for he was thick about the middle and hard put to make haste. "Anyone would think you've been evading me, lord!"

A well-to-do merchant of wool and specialty goods, Gruffydd was the envy of many. Yet despite his coveted wealth, humble Welsh origins seemed to cause him perpetual embarrassment. He was prickly as a nettle patch and wary always of slights alluding to his lowly roots, real or imagined. "Nay, it's not so, Master Gruffydd. I've been occupied with fair business."

"Of course, my lord," he said. "Forgive me."

Godwin, surprised by the easy capitulation, peered more closely at the merchant, noting a sagging mouth and red-rimmed eyes. Despite the midday heat, Gruffydd sported a rich cape, yet seemed oddly diminished by the sumptuous drapery, looking like a turtle poking a tentative head from its grandly protective shell.

"It's about the guild feast, my Lord. I wanted to remind you that the officers will be meeting tonight to discuss the final details. You will attend won't you? You hadn't forgotten again?"

He had forgotten. Though not an officer of Hexham's guild, an association dedicated to St. Wilfrid, Godwin was a patron. And as bailiff, he was obligated to attend all town meetings as the archbishop's representative. Regretfully, he could not avoid tonight's gathering. He thought of Asheferth and felt a stab of envy.

The annual guild feast was the fellowship's most momentous occasion. Godwin knew that Gruffydd, as the guild's steward, had devoted months of planning to ensure its success, to see that it was imbued with all the pomp and ceremony he could muster. "Of course I'll be there, Master Gruffydd," he said, thinking he could slip away for a game of chess with Brother Elias. "In the Chapter House as usual? And the time?"

"Compline," Gruffydd said. "It will be brief, lord. We have only to go over a few matters: the order of procession and seating. . . ." The merchant's eyes slid away, his face flushing.

Godwin quickly surmised that reminder of last year's

brawl embarrassed him. The order of procession into the refectory and seating were determined by rank. The fraternity's three noble patrons, Lord Godwin, Lady Constance, and Lord Acomb, would proceed first to take their seats upon a raised dais. Knights and gentry followed, but the order of the officers was more difficult to settle, and last year an unseemly altercation had broken out when some learned of their places. The dispute grew quite heated, and Godwin was forced to break up the fighting after Master Gruffydd failed, getting his nose broken in the process.

"We'll choose by lot to avoid any . . . hard feelings among our guild officers," Gruffydd added.

"Very wise, Master Gruffydd."

Godwin waited as the merchant continued to stand awkwardly by, although their business had been concluded. "Well, until tonight."

"My lord," Gruffydd said, "Could I speak with you privately? When it's convenient of course—"

"Lord Godwin!" a deep voice boomed over the jostling crowd. He turned to see his deputy Wulfstan hastening toward him. As always, he was dressed for battle, or knightly sport, wearing a mail hauberk and leggings. He stopped before the bailiff, hand poised on the hilt of his sheathed sword.

"What is it Wulfstan?" Godwin asked, no longer alarmed by his deputy's dramatic appearances, having learned that Wulfstan reported all happenings in the same manner, whether it be news of a raid or the birth of a babe.

"It is your mother, Lady Gunnilda. She has arrived at Dilston Hall and bids you to come welcome her."

Godwin nodded, turning back to address Gruffydd. But the merchant was already lumbering away, heavy cape outlining his slumping shoulders.

TWO ✠

Lady Constance of Bordweal Manor waited as her women settled themselves on benches scattered throughout the orchard. As they took up their spindle whorls and distaffs and small bundles of unspun wool, she drew a large book to her lap and opened it to "Yves and Nicolette," a romance. She had promised them a knightly tale this time, not a psalm or another saint's life, but a chivalrous story of love and adventure. She waited for the idle talk to subside, for the chirps and trilling of the younger women—punctuated by low clucks from their elders—to grow silent.

One eventide at midsummer, she began, translating French to English, *King Arthur held a splendid court at his castle in Cardigan, attended by many proud knights, noble ladies, and fair maidens. The king told his knights that he wished to hunt the white stag, to renew the observance of that venerable tradition. "Brave knights, tomorrow we shall go to the forest where adventures abound. We shall hunt the white stag! It will be glorious, and each of you shall prove your worth to knighthood and the ladies."*

At dawn the next day, the king arose and dressed, donning a short tunic for riding in the forest. He had his knights wakened and the horses made ready. Soon they were mounted and on their way, a great company hastening to the forest. Spurring hard after them came another knight of the Round Table. His name was Yves, a proud and handsome man. . . .

THREE ✠

The babe was eager to be born. Three women kneeled beside Agnes as she writhed mutely on the straw pallet, her small fists gripping the bedclothes. She could not bring forth the child. Constance wrung a cloth from a mazer of cool water and pressed it to Agnes's cheeks. "The labor quickens," she said as the woman heaved and tossed with renewed vigor, her breathing coming in quick, shallow pants. Body and coverlet were drenched.

"Aye, lady, and no sign of the babe," the midwife said. She was peering between Agnes's twisting thighs, trying to keep them in an arched position. A frown marked her large, plain face as she chanted softly, *"Acre arcre arnem nona aernem bedor nidren acrun cunad ele harassan fidine."*

Hafren then motioned for Cynwyse to come closer and, keeping her voice low, told the cook, "Fetch wild parsnip from my shed. You'll find the roots in a basket near the door. Choose a large one and boil it up with like parts of milk and water. The broth may hasten the babe from the womb."

Constance followed her cook from the lying-in "chamber." Not a separate room, in truth, for Agnes's toft was only a tiny cottage. The thin wattle and daub partition marking off the private space accommodated little more than the narrow cot upon which the woman strained. Yet the dwelling was clean and sturdy, built this season by her husband in anticipation of their first child.

"I'll go after the herb, Cynwyse," Constance said. "Hafren may need help and you have more skill than I."

"Aye, yer right on that score, lady," she said, her worn face puckered with worry. "Many a bairn I've helped into the world, but I've never seen one tarry so in the womb." She moved to the hearth and stirred the coals to kindle a flame. "'Twas Lauds when her pains started," she said, adding small chips of kindling to fuel the fire, "and by Prime she was bearin' down nicely. Now it's past Vespers—when ye came, lady—and still Agnes labors." She put a tripod in the fire and set a small cauldron of water on it. As Constance started for the door, Cynwyse called after, "Bring rosemary, too, lady—for luck."

Constance hastened from the cottage, passing into the long light of a late summer evening. Agnes and Bethoc lived halfway along a narrow road that served a stretch of peasant smallholdings. Adjacent to the lane were the strips of land they cultivated as free tenants of Bordweal Manor. As she hurried toward Hafren's croft, Constance saw several of her freeholders mingling in their gardens and closes. Many cheerfully haled her, while a few ducked their heads or offered a bow. They had lost Lord Aidan on crusade two years past, and his young widow now stood in his stead until their son, Aldwin, just three years old, grew to claim his manhood and patrimony.

As Constance rushed by the new haystacks, she saw a small face peeking from a loose pile of straw. The children were playing at hide-and-seek, she realized with a brief smile. In fact, all were taking their ease, for the grain harvest was in, the stalks flailed and husks winnowed. The precious wheat had been put by in sacks hanging from cottage rafters. Now was the pleasant interval before the final ingathering of ripened corn and apples by Michaelmas; time for the sweet pleasures offered by a waning summer and by Hexham's

August fair. She prayed Agnes and her babe would share in the joy.

Hafren and her husband, Gothard, were among the more prosperous of Constance's tenants, as the size of their farmstead confirmed. It was situated at the end of the lane, a bit removed from the others. A longhouse, large garden, barn, and shed sat contentedly on a generous croft, neatly squared and enclosed by willow pickets. The big, glad family lived closest to Bordweal, their croft hard by her manor's orchard.

Hafren had brought her husband a small dowry and even more in the way of prestige, for she hailed from local gentry, though a family rather strained in its holdings. The two daughters had been married off to decent suitors—not noble, but respectable men—while one son received what was left of the family's dwindling riches.

Her children were at play in the close, and when Constance came through the gate, they ran toward her with peals of joy, for she usually carried treats for the children. "Lady Constance! Lady Constance!" They gathered to her like bees. Little Isabel thrust a posy of bruised flowers at her, saying, "These are for *you!*"

"Thank you, angel," Constance said, taking the battered flowers. "Who's minding you?" she asked the upturned faces, noticing that baby Mary was attempting to climb into a tub of water. Constance hurried over to scoop her up as she nearly toppled in.

"*Me*, lady," declared eight-year-old Cecelia.

"Nay, *I* am," countered her twin sister, Alice.

"Aunt Maegden said *I* am to look after my sisters, not you—"

"Where is your aunt, then?" Constance interrupted. But the twins only shrugged. When she pressed them again she learned that Maegden, Hafren's younger sister, had come earlier to help with their baths.

"There is to be a great feast at the manor tomorrow," Cecelia told her, as if Constance mightn't have known.

"And the fair starts the day after *that!*" Alice piped in.

"Where's your da, then?" Constance asked.

"Oh, he's taking the flock from the hay-meadow to the wheat fields."

She quickly led them over to the garden where she saw daisies growing thick among the beans, telling them to sit in a circle. "You'll want garlands for your hair when you come to my feast." Tearing out a clump of flowers, then another, she tossed them into the ring of laughing girls—Isabel, the twins, Felicia, Hanna, and Elena—and left them happily plaiting. Hafren had thus far produced only one boy, Duncan, who was no doubt helping his father in the fields.

With Mary on her hip, she went to the shed, sending hens and fatted capons scurrying from her path. Inside, she set the baby on a pile of rushes and found the basket of parsnip roots, pulling forth several from a tangled collection. Next, she found bunches of dried rosemary hanging from a beam. Its keen scent filled the shed as she handled the herb, pushing sprigs into the sleeve of her gown along with Isabel's posy.

"Come, Mary." But the baby was already tottering through the doorway in pursuit of an alarmed hen. Constance took her up once again, though she protested this time, crying with arms outstretched toward the chicken, which, sensing the threat had passed, resumed its placid pecking. Constance hurried across the close and through the gate, making her way to Hafren's closest neighbor, Ebba. Her daughter Hilda was a servant at Bordweal, nanny for Constance's son. Ebba was taking advantage of the fine evening by gathering onions. Would she mind Hafren's children until their father or Maegden returned? "Aye, lady," the sweet-natured woman replied, taking the baby into her arms. "How is Agnes?"

"Not well," Constance said before hastening off. She was finally returning to the cottage when she saw Bethoc coming from the fields, waving his arm. He drew up breathlessly and offered a quick bow, asking, "How does my Agnes, lady?" He was a tall man and nut-brown from fieldwork.

Carefully, Constance said, "She labors still, Bethoc, but we're preparing a broth that may hasten the babe along."

He frowned, arms dangling awkwardly. "She must be sore weary, my girl."

"Aye, but Agnes is strong. God willing, she'll bring forth the babe soon." She put a hand to the latch. "I must see to the broth. Come inside, why don't you?"

"Nay," he said, shrinking back, either at the impropriety of her suggestion or reluctant to hear his wife suffer.

Constance handed the roots over to Cynwyse who inspected them carefully. "Aye, it's wild parsnip." She deftly minced the largest, placing the pulp into a milk and water mixture already simmering on the hearth.

"How is she?" But Constance already knew the answer, for the woman's hard breathing, hoarse with strain and weariness, filled the cottage. It was dimly lit, with door and shutters closed tight against the dusky evening light, keeping Agnes's struggles private. In a corner stood a newly carved cradle. Constance went over to it and offered up another prayer to St. Margaret, placing the sprigs of rosemary on its tiny coverlet.

"No different," Cynwyse said, shaking her gray head. She was straining the broth through a square of clean cloth.

Agnes only managed small sips of the decoction, but it seemed to help, for it was not long before she finally brought her first babe into the world. When the crown of its head appeared, she gave one last wrenching shriek, then collapsed onto her back as the baby slipped out into the midwife's waiting hands.

He was big and hale, judging by his squawks of protest. When the cord was tied off and cut, Cynwyse carried him to a warm bath near the hearth, while Hafren prepared for the last of the labor. Constance bathed Agnes's white face once again, telling the new mother, "He is beautiful. And strong willed. Hear how he complains about his first bath!"

But Agnes seemed unaware of her lady. Constance thought the new mother had drifted into an exhausted slumber until she saw Hafren working desperately to stem a tide of blood flowing from the womb.

Calmly, the midwife instructed, "Lady, we need more straw, a good deal. And any rags you can muster."

Constance ran from the chamber and returned with a tall basket of clean rushes. She pulled out big wads, handing them to Hafren, who called to Cynwyse, "Bring the babe and put him to nurse."

Constance started to object. Was it wise to further tax Agnes's strength? But she said nothing, for Hafren knew her business.

Cynwyse held the baby to its mother's breast, and he suckled eagerly. Hafren massaged Agnes's lower stomach, keeping her eyes on the flow of blood. No longer conscious, the new mother's face was slack, pale, and cool to the touch. A bolt of fear shot through Constance. "Hafren," she whispered, "should I fetch a priest?"

She answered tersely, "Nay, lady, I think not." She kept massaging and soaking up blood with straw. It was quiet, the only sound that of the baby nursing.

"But shouldn't we be prepared? Her immortal soul—"

"I can chant the rites, if the need is desperate —but look, the bleeding is slowing."

Finally, it stopped altogether, though Agnes continued to dwell in a still slumber, and Constance wondered uneasily again whether they ought to send for Brother Elias. "She's wrought hard all day," Hafren said. "Rest is the best potion now."

They bundled Agnes in a blanket while Cynwyse took the contented baby to his cradle near the hearth. Hafren, bent and tired, came over to admire him. "Ach! he's plump as a butter cake!"

Constance opened the cottage door to find Bethoc hovering. "Come see your son," she beckoned. She left it standing open, for the breeze was mild and clean, carrying with it the sweet song of an evening thrush.

Bethoc went first to the cradle, peering in cautiously. "A

big lad," he said, smiling proudly. He went to Agnes next, standing over her for several minutes. When he returned to the hearth, he asked Hafren, "Will she mend?"

"Aye, I think so. But Agnes will be feeble for a time, not fit t'care for a new babe and husband."

"Her sister's not far," he said. "And there's help aplenty nearby."

"I'll come again in the morning, but fetch me if she worsens, no matter the hour."

"I'll come, too," Cynwyse said. "A powerful potion have I for Agnes. 'Twill make her strong again. She'll be comin' on nicely before ye knows it."

When they left, he was standing uncertainly between cradle and wife.

The Compline bell was ringing in the hour as the women walked toward the manor house. Constance went a little ahead of Hafren and Cynwyse, who walked slowly behind, heads bent in quiet conversation. She was worried for Agnes. What if she should die in the night, unshriven? Then, as she passed the burned-out remains of the old parish church, it occurred to Constance that she ought to have it rebuilt; for in dire situations, the priory cathedral in Hexham might be too far for the swift retrieval of a priest.

She had no idea when the stone chapel had been destroyed; it being long before her arrival in Hexhamshire four years ago. All at Bordweal seemed long accustomed to attending mass at the priory cathedral. A pleasant walk or ride in good weather, down the gentle slopes of the Tyne valley to the bridge and up the opposite hillside to Hexham. But when in haste, when every moment counted, or when the weather was foul, the journey might be too long.

Yes, she would talk to her steward tomorrow about rebuilding the chapel. He would object to the expense, of course, but she would insist. Why had the idea not occurred to her before? she wondered. And a priest would be needed as well. One of the canons from the priory perhaps? She dismissed the thought immediately. Brother Elias was the only fit canon at St. Andrews, and he was its acting prior.

Constance arrived at Hafren's gate. All was quiet, and she wondered if Maegden had returned to care for her nieces. She waited as Cynwyse and Hafren drew up, still deep in conversation, the midwife nodding at something the cook was saying. When Cynwyse saw her mistress, she said, "Ach, don't take on so, lady! Agnes will mend, we'll see t'that!" She put a strong arm around Constance and gave her shoulders a shake.

Hafren said nothing. The midwife was spent, her face drawn. She was only a year or two older than Constance, but she looked much older. Putting a hand to the gate, she saw Constance studying her. "Aye, I think she'll come 'round. 'Twas a close brush, though. I can't deny that."

Constance said, "Have you . . . lost many in childbirth, Hafren?" Her own had been fairly easy and the few others she had witnessed had been nothing like Agnes's ordeal.

"To be sure," she said, shaking her head. "Ten years I've been midwifing. Many a death I've seen, babes and mothers both."

They stood silently under the darkening sky. " 'Tisn't like the stories you read to us is it, lady?" Hafren added. "Life can take a cruel turn and bring no happy ending."

"Aye," Cynwyse agreed. "It has its storms, some deadly. But often we come through t'find a new beginning, just as the stories tell." The cook held Constance's eyes, adding, "Ye must take hold of the chance before it passes."

FOUR ✝

The journey from Hexham to Dilston Hall was always a pleasant one for Godwin. He could cover the distance in just under an hour using the east highway, a tract through sparsely settled farmland and deep brakes of oak and hazel. Keeping to higher ground, the road runs fairly straight, dipping from time to time into narrow glens and thickets. Dusky, secret places these, said to be the haunts of fairy families, perilous to those who stray from the road. Or, if one heeds the tales of the troubadours, it is here that an adventure-seeking knight can find his greatest challenge and the lady of his dreams.

Within these dells, Godwin thought it more likely to stumble upon a den of highwaymen than brownies, and he always proceeded warily. Nor would he allow his twelve-year-old nephew and helpmate, Eilaf, now accompanying him, to travel the road alone. But reports of highway thievery in the shire were rare these days, the bailiff was proud to acknowledge, for his household retinue routinely patrolled the main routes into Hexham. Still, he would take no chances with his sister's son.

Bosa was there as well. He trailed behind, as he was wont to do on quiet woodland tracts. During these times, his young deputy retreated into a daydream world, and Godwin often wondered who or what peopled it. Knights, castles, ladies? Pixies and white harts? Perhaps nothing more fanciful than a small croft on a fertile square of earth.

Gentle Bosa was colossal in size with a heart to match and ill-suited for his rank as deputy. This mattered not to his father, who stubbornly insisted that Bosa exercise his knightly inheritance.

"Uncle," Eilaf said, "did *you* know grandmother was coming?" They were entering the woods surrounding Dilston Hall, going a bit slower than Godwin's usual pace for the sake of Eilaf's pony, a dwarf next to his mighty stallion. Godwin did not mind, enjoying the cool and quiet of the forest and the earthy fragrance of decayed leaves layered upon the woodland floor. Afternoon birdsong echoed in the treetops, spinning a web of sweet melodies. Above all could be heard the solitary song of the thrush, a call that never failed to stir a longing in Godwin. He said, "We never know when she's coming nephew, nor how long she might stay. She comes and goes as she likes."

Godwin's mother, Lady Gunnilda, had been a widow for thirty-four years. Despite many offers and efforts on the part of her brother, the Earl, to cement an ally through a wedding with his sister, she steadfastly maintained her solitary life.

She had established for herself an itinerant lifestyle, alighting with a household entourage at her dower lands in Wingates, at the Earl's court in Dunbar, here at Dilston Hall, or wherever desire took her. Last year she had attended at Canterbury the solemn translation of Thomas Becket. On several occasions, she had traveled abroad on pilgrimages to Santiago and Rome, where the pope politely declined to meet with her, despite Gunnilda's numerous overtures. At the beginning of this summer, she had traveled with her brother Earl Patric and King Alexander's royal household to York, where Scotland's king wed Joan, the eldest sister of England's boy-king, Henry.

"I wish I could go with her," Eilaf said, hastening to add, "I want most of all to serve you, Uncle, only sometimes . . . I think it would be exciting to see other places."

"Well, why not?" Godwin said. "It's easy enough to arrange, and it would give her pleasure to have you at her side. She adores you," he teased, knowing Eilaf was embarrassed by his grandmother's affection.

Eilaf grinned and squirmed in his saddle. "She kisses and hugs me!"

"Aye, you must indulge her," Godwin said, laughing. At twelve, Eilaf was lanky, growing by the day it seemed. Or stretching more like, for the taller he got, the more slender he became. He was not awkward, like others his age, and there was strength in his narrow limbs. Godwin watched as he sat easily upon his mount, body moving in rhythm with the beast's gait, hands held loosely about the reins. "Your grandmother misses you when she's abroad. You're her only grandchild."

"Not for long! Mother's with child and father's sure it is another son!"

Godwin nodded, remembering his last conversation with William, Eilaf's father. "Every man needs at least two sons— an heir and a spare!" After a good snort and guffaw, William added, nudging Godwin, "Time to get busy yourself, brother-in-law!"

"I couldn't go away with Grandmother," Eilaf said. "Father wouldn't allow it. He wants me here, serving you, learning to be a knight."

Godwin didn't want to think about the day when he might gird a sword about Eilaf's waist and send him into the world. "You are many years from knighthood. There is time enough to learn the ways of sword and armor. What's more, journeying is a kind of schooling —the best, I think.

Eilaf gave this some thought. "If you go, too, Father *couldn't* object. Will you, Uncle? And Bosa must come, of course." He turned in the saddle to check on the progress of his friend.

Godwin was surprised by the stirrings Eilaf's words prompted. He had not enjoyed such feelings in a long while, not since he had taken the cross three years ago with his cousin, Aidan. He felt a longing to ride the moors, to camp in the wild with his boon companions, to seek hospitality in the halls of kin.

But his answer was, "I have duties here, nephew, law to keep. I cannot depart on a whim as Grandmother might. But I give you leave to go. Your father will not oppose me."

Eilaf's expression said otherwise. "When father came last, he was angry. I handled his horse and gear poorly."

Godwin remembered. Poor Eilaf had been drilled relentlessly, and while he did the same tasks for Godwin with grace and ease, with his father bearing down he became clumsy and inept. William was furious. "What's he been doing all this time?" he bellowed at Godwin. "He has never lifted a blade, by the look of it!"

"Of course, he hasn't! He's just a boy, William, not a soldier." Godwin's sister, Egfrida, stood anxiously by, wringing her hands as always.

"I must work harder," Eilaf said, but without enthusiasm. Godwin had noticed lately that his nephew was showing forced interest in horses and weapons. On the other hand, he was excelling at his studies. The tutor Godwin employed had complained the other day, somewhat shamefacedly, that Eilaf was demanding of the schoolmaster more than he could provide.

"When will I learn to handle a sword, Uncle?"

"Soon. But first I think your reading and writing skills need attention."

Eilaf looked quickly at Godwin.

"If Brother Elias is willing, perhaps it is time to move your studies to St. Andrews."

Eilaf wore a big smile. "Father will not like it."

"Let me worry about that."

"Godwin!" his mother exclaimed when they entered the hall. She was seated before a roaring fire, despite the August heat. Her feet were bare, blue leather shoes tossed carelessly aside, her woolen hose little bundles of fine fabric beneath the bench. With short, plump legs outstretched, Gunnilda was wiggling her pink toes at the flames.

Godwin went to her, laughing. "How I've missed you!" she said, holding him with unexpected strength. Then she looked past Godwin. "My grandson!" And it was Eilaf's turn. He gave in to her affections, but not before giving Godwin a long-suffering look. Bosa received a hearty embrace too, for Gunnilda had taken to him as another grandson, and he favored her with his big grin.

All around servants scurried. Gunnilda's numerous trunks had been brought into the hall, and now her practiced staff, supervised by her long-time steward, Duff, worked to put everything in its proper place. Godwin pulled a bench close to his mother while Eilaf and Bosa drifted toward the kitchens. "You look well, Mother." And indeed she did— round and dimpled, beaming and content. "You have just come from Dunbar?"

"Aye, my son. Patric sends you greetings and desires your presence at court when duties allow."

"I'll go when I can, but it won't be soon I'd wager. The fair is upon us, the harvest next. And somehow I must find time to look over my lands in the north."

Eilaf and Bosa strolled back into the hall, cradling apples. Eilaf perched on the hearth, while Bosa lowered his bulk nearby, handing two apples to Godwin. The three proceeded to munch noisily.

"You *would* be free to tend your lands *and* favor your uncle were you not keeper of a hamlet." It was becoming a familiar reproach, as Gunnilda grew increasingly frustrated with her son's desire to remain Bailiff of Hexhamshire.

Around a mouthful of apple Godwin said, "But I am, so why act as if I mightn't be?"

Servants came into the hall to erect the trestle tables for supper. Benches were hauled over, the tables laid with plates and knives. "You will grow weary of the post sooner or later, Godwin. Why not sooner? Why serve that Angevin, Walter de Gray? You needn't serve any! But if you so choose, serve for honor and wealth. Patric is kin and has plenty of both to dispense!"

She had obviously been chewing on her thoughts for some time to have them out so quickly. Or was Patric behind it? Eilaf was attentively taking in the exchange. "I will ponder your words, Mother. But come, get you dressed! Supper is ready."

Gunnilda did not rise, saying, "There is more news from Dunbar, distressing tidings I'm afraid. Lord Eilan met with an accident while hunting—a stray arrow pierced his shoulder. He'll mend, I have no doubt. The man is iron! Still, my sister is in agony, and Earl Patric is very worried."

Godwin frowned. "Has word been sent to Bordweal?" Lord Eilan was Constance's father-in-law. The two had formed a strong bond when Aidan, the beloved son and husband, died on crusade.

"Yes, I sent a messenger myself."

He nodded, thinking he would send his own to Dunbar in the morning to learn the latest tidings.

Gunnilda suddenly grasped his hand, saying, "Return with me to Dunbar. Your presence will speed Eilan's recovery, I know it!"

He held her hand within both of his. "My uncle is as stalwart as a fortress. He'll mend whether I'm there or no. Now come, Mother, supper is growing cold."

Gunnilda was seated at the head of the largest table where she liked to preside with Godwin on her right, Eilaf to her left, and next to him, Bosa. Duff stood attentively at his mistress's side. As the former steward of Dilston Hall, he tended to resume these duties when Gunnilda visited. Bony and tall, he was growing stoop-shouldered, Godwin noticed with some concern. Yet his neighborly face and gamesome, hazel eyes under a tangle of white brows were as constant as ever. His father's steward, Duff was born when the north still belonged to Scotland's King David and his son, Prince

Henry. He had stories aplenty to tell, and Godwin had heard them all.

Several of his household knights ambled in, trailing helpmates and assorted hounds. Asheferth, Godwin noted, was not among them. They clambered noisily over the benches, tucking in with enthusiasm, rocking the tables in their haste. Gunnilda pursed her lips and stared hard at Godwin, demanding a rebuke. But he only asked for wine, and Duff promptly filled their cups. Platters of food arrived from the kitchen and before long the hall was filled with the sounds of men and boys attending their appetites.

After a while, Gunnilda stopped her delicate nibbling to lean forward and lay a hand on Godwin's arm, "My son, is it not time again to take a wife?" She kept her voice low, but Eilaf caught her words and smirked into his pork pie. Duff looked elsewhere. Godwin chewed a hunk of bread, ignoring the question. This was another topic that was becoming tediously familiar. Gunnilda continued doggedly, despite her son's silence. "A woman's presence is what this manor needs. Look about you. There is no gentlewoman here but me! A gracious wife makes a genial household. And a clean one," she added, clucking her tongue as she glanced around the room.

It was a small hall compared to most manors the size of Dilston, something Godwin liked, for it made an inviting setting. Overhead, the great beams and struts wove a wooden canopy, the timbers dark and smoky with age. The hall *was* clean, but only just, he suddenly noticed. The rushes could do with changing, the greasy woodwork scrubbing. He observed a pile of broken crockery in one corner. It had been growing, he realized, without anyone bothering to remove the shards. His knights sometimes grew careless with the tableware, especially when the wine and ale had made several passes.

A jug of wine crashed to the floor, echoing his thoughts. Chadd shouted to a serving girl, who scurried over and bent to retrieve the broken pieces, nimbly dodging the knight's hands. She laughed coquettishly and danced out of his reach, tossing the pottery on the pile. She went off to the kitchens, hips swaying for Chadd's benefit. Eilaf stared after the maid, slack-jawed. Bosa, oblivious, kept his eyes on his plate, dishing in victuals.

"Yes, I see your point, Mother. The men have become a bit coarse and myself lax. I'll speak to my knights and ask the steward to hire another cleaning girl."

"No! Not another servant, Godwin, a wife!"

Everyone stopped their wolfing to stare at mother and son. Then they nudged each other, grinning, and started the ale around again.

"A competent wife brings efficiency to a household," she lectured, lowering her voice. "Dilston has plenty of servants, more than it ought. They could be worked harder, but there is no one to oversee them save your steward, and he is stretched to the limit with you in Hexham day after day. Ask Duff, he will say the same." But before the steward could offer a reply, Gunnilda hastened on. "A noble woman inspires virtuous behavior. Your men would soon mend their rude ways."

Godwin pointed a drumstick at her, "*Your* presence doesn't seem to make a difference, Mother."

"Of course not," she snorted. "I'm old and fat. A *young* wife will stir them to gallantry."

"They shall be stirred all right. So I'm to dangle the tasty morsel of my wife as bait?" Godwin winked at Eilaf and waited.

Gunnilda's chubby fist slammed the table, though the gesture was barely heard so lively was the hall now. "You deliberately misunderstand my meaning—"

She stopped suddenly, looking from son to grandson, and then let out a hearty cackle. "You mock me, wicked son!" She shook a finger at him, "But you know I speak the truth. There is Lady Constance—"

"Grandmother," Eilaf interrupted, "Uncle Godwin is moving my studies to the priory." He had been observing their conversation with great interest. Never had he known anyone to speak so imperiously to his uncle, yet illicit nothing more than a laugh or a promise to consider her words. Often, he thought she went *too* far and wondered why his uncle tolerated it. Impulsively, he decided to weigh in and deflect her assault.

Gunnilda turned to rest her gaze on him, knowing exactly what he was up to. Eilaf braced for a scolding. However, she said nothing, only turned back to look at her son, raising an eyebrow. Godwin shrugged.

"What a grand idea!" she finally said, a gleam in her eye. "Though I fear William will not think so." Eilaf remembered his father and was immediately despondent. "Be not troubled, Grandson," she assured him, shaking his narrow shoulder. "Uncle Godwin will make your father see reason. And I, too, shall put in a word." Eilaf brightened instantly and Godwin chuckled. William was terrified of his mother-in-law.

After supper, to Gunnilda's consternation, Godwin returned to Hexham. There was the guild meeting to attend, and he wanted to inspect the fair site once more, as well as meet with Wulfstan. Gunnilda's mouth tightened when Godwin told her he would be staying the night in the Moot Hall, but she said nothing, and he left her in the company of Eilaf and Bosa.

He took a fresh mount to spare Saedraca another journey and arrived in Hexham in time to meet with his deputy before the guild meeting at the priory. He stabled the beast and went to the tavern where he knew Wulfstan would be, given the hour.

The inn was bustling. New and old faces mingled over ale as merchants and tradesmen slaked thirsts and appetites after a long day on the road. Two fiddlers worked the cramped space for pennies. Alone in a corner sat an old man.

Wulfstan was sitting in another corner, back to the wall,

eyes narrowed on the crowd. Even when he raised his cup to drink, they glittered over the rim like two points of candlelight. He made a very good deputy, if excessively enthusiastic. Godwin retrieved a mug of ale and sat to hear Wulfstan's report.

There were a few complaints of thievery already—one serious. A cask of wine had been stolen from a boat moored along the bridge. "The merchant's screaming for justice," Wulfstan sneered, as if the man had no right.

"Well, we'd better give it to him. How does a cask disappear from a moored boat in daylight without anyone seeing who took it?"

Wulfstan shrugged. Speculation was not his strongest suit. "I sent Burchard and Osbern." Godwin nodded and his deputy continued, "Matthew Tanner is letting out his rooms to harlots again."

"How many?"

"Two. Easy enough to spot. He's says they are kin from Morpeth."

"Escort them to the border."

Locals did all they could to share in the profits offered by fairgoers. They provided food, entertainment, lodging, anything for extra silver. And every year, one or two brothels sprang up. Harlots were forbidden from fairs because of the threat they posed to fairgoers and residents. They were classed with roadside garbage heaps, lepers, and insufficient water supplies for fighting fires. Godwin rarely arrested prostitutes unless they proved to be thieves as well, as experience had shown they could be.

"Who's the old man?" Godwin nodded at the corner.

"Calls himself a leech, a man of medicine."

"A leech," Godwin repeated slowly. He'd never known one to attend Hexham's fair.

"Aye, from York. He's rented a booth, all proper like. He has many books—big ones." Wulfstan's lip curled. He had no use for reading and writing. Recognizing the seal of a relevant individual was learned enough for Wulfstan.

"The justices from York have arrived," he went on, dismissing the leech. "They're settling in at the priory."

Godwin swallowed the last of his ale, looking once more in the direction of the leech. His journey had obviously taxed him, for he was staring vacantly across the room. The gown he wore was coarse and unadorned, a mere sack thrown over skeletal limbs. He noticed Godwin's gaze and stared back, gaunt face giving his eyes a wild look.

"Well done, Wulfstan," Godwin said, turning back to his deputy. They went over the rotation of guards next. Eight were stationed at the fair site, another ten patrolled the roads. Godwin told him about Asheferth. "We'll have one less knight, I'm afraid."

"A boon that," his deputy growled. "He's as fell as a sparrowhawk and no use to me."

"Aye, he's wild," Godwin agreed. "But I recall another fell knight who entered my service some years back. Not so bad did *he* turn out." Wulfstan stared a moment, then barked out his amusement as the bell for Compline began to ring.

Godwin was late to the guild meeting, for though the tavern was in the Market Square and only steps from the priory gatehouse, he was stopped several times to answer an assortment of queries. It was a relief to finally gain entry to St. Andrews and stroll its quiet grounds to the Chapter House.

Hexham is no large town, home to a handful of free craftsmen and the same number of merchants. What set it apart, besides its annual fair, was the priory cathedral. Built by St. Wilfrid ages past, St. Andrews was the heart of the town. Firmly fixed in its midst, the cathedral presided over the Market Square, yet remained aloof, set apart by a high stone wall that encircled the church, its various houses and a large precinct of meadow and garden. Entrance was through its imposing gatehouse.

The meeting was tedious, as Godwin knew it would be, with the town elite bickering over every matter. To Godwin's disappointment, Brother Elias was away inspecting the abbey's corn mills at Hamburn. As a result, the cathedral was very quiet, for with the acting prior away, the monks were dispensing with the hours, and no liturgy was sung for Compline.

Godwin propped himself out of the way on the cold stone seat that ringed the Chapter House and nodded off. Gruffydd left him in peace, save only when the bailiff was needed to rule on a point in dispute. Finally it was over, and Godwin made his way wearily from the gatehouse to the Market Square and then across the stone paving to the Moot Hall, thinking only of the thick feather mattress in its loft.

The Moot Hall served as his headquarters—a stout, rather ugly structure in contrast to the cathedral. He had just drifted to sleep when a sound brought him suddenly awake. Godwin lay in the dark, listening. Had it been a dream? No, it was the sound of a key turning in the lock. He heard the oak door of the Moot Hall slowly swing open. Quietly, he reached for his leather breeches, pulling them on. Then he remained still, listening. A man's voice, familiar, murmured below, and Godwin's tense body relaxed. It was Asheferth. He was about to call out when he heard another voice, a woman's, speak softly. It, too, was familiar, but high and sweet like a choirboy's.

Something kept him from charging down the ladder, and he sat indecisively on the edge of his pallet. Then he heard the rustle of fabric and the chink of armor. Their breathing quickened and Godwin desperately sought a way out of the predicament. The woman moaned and Asheferth's response was hoarse and urgent. There was an eager fumbling of garments as Godwin looked around wildly, spying his sword propped against the wall. With his foot, he sent it clattering to the floor. Below, startled whispers, silence, and then sounds of the couple quietly stealing away. Godwin dropped onto the bed, laughing shakily. He would have to have a talk with Asheferth. He went hunting all right!

FIVE ✝

On the eve of the fair's opening, Constance held a feast for the tenants and peasant families of Bordweal. Most would not be attending the guild feast the following evening, for the fellowship's annual gala was largely a town affair. But she wanted her own folk to share in the revelries and so had arranged Bordweal's first fair eve feast.

She was sitting alone beneath a tree at the edge of the orchard where she could observe both the festivities and newcomers. The merrymaking had begun a short while ago beneath a fine August sky when a piper and his acrobat wife rang in the entertainment. The children had stared in open-mouthed wonder as Matilda "Makejoy" merrily flipped and tumbled to the tune of the bagpipe. They immediately set out to duplicate her antics, and the meadow was now alive with leaping, rolling, whirling, and twisting youngsters. The acrobat happily instructed while her husband Tom "Playatune" piped one gay tune after another. They were humble folk, these, not the disdainful, sought-after minstrels who performed at court.

From time to time Constance looked across the sloping hills beyond the manor for a rider. But mostly she watched her son as he cavorted with the rest of the children. She laughed when she saw little Cecelia earnestly instructing him in the execution of a somersault, her garland of wilted daisies cocked to one side like a crooked halo. To her frustration and to Aldwin's immense delight, he kept flopping to one side instead of rolling straight forward.

Her son's features were those of his father—a narrowly sculpted face, shapely and refined, though he was only three years old. His eyes were wide, dark, and bright. But in build he took after another. Godwin said it was his grandfather, Lord Eilan, and Constance agreed. Solid and stocky, Aldwin's stout, swift legs took him in a flash wherever desire called. He was quicker than a greyhound, keeping Constance, Cynwyse, and Hilda on constant vigil. Thinking of Lord Eilan brought a stab of worry, though the messenger said her father-in-law was mending.

Her eyes moved from Aldwin to the entire gathering: the conversations, the music, and the children. She hoped her fair eve feast would become an annual event, like the harvest home feast, or the Whitsun celebrations.

Constance was doing this frequently now—offering new ideas, reforming old ways—and she knew her steward, Hereberht, didn't quite know what to make of it. Always inscrutable, it was impossible to perceive his true thoughts, but she knew him well enough to sense mixed feelings. He disapproved of her increasing involvement in the running of Bordweal, yet seemed relieved that she was once again taking an interest. He resented the intrusion, but grudgingly approved if her suggestions were useful.

But Hereberht did *not* approve of spreading wealth, and many of Constance's proposals involved just that, like the new chapel and today's feast. Austere to the point of asceticism, he owned two plain gowns and was as taut as good rope. He never voiced his displeasure and again she sensed a conflict. He accepted her desire to directly oversee the duties associated with Aldwin's guardianship. This she did gladly, indeed, it was all that had kept her from complete despair in the early days of widowhood. But now she wanted more. Bordweal was her home, too, and she wanted to better this place, to be a part of it. But when Constance had proposed the new chapel, he grew stiff, more so than usual, drawing himself up into a rigid pillar of censure. But there was more to it than silver, for he had struck the same pose when he found her with Sidroc, learning the ways of bees, and yesterday when she assisted Hafren and Cynwyse with the birthing.

She did not worry overmuch, though. No steward was as trusty and loyal as hers. Hereberht may not agree with her decisions, but he would not challenge them, at least not directly. Constance noticed that he was becoming adept at mitigating their impact, as with today's feast. He had instructed the freeholders to bring a plate of food, if they could manage it, or a faggot of wood for tonight's bonfire. What Hereberht didn't know is that many of these contributions were going to Agnes and Bethoc.

The new mother was still bedridden and would be for at least a fortnight. Cynwyse had gone around first thing to give her a healing potion—a concoction of water drawn from the blacksmith's cooling trough mixed with mallow leaves—and had reported to Constance that Agnes was improving, though she tired easily. On the other hand, the new baby was hearty and spirited. "Kept his da up all night," she chuckled. "But he's a-sleepin' like a top now." The baby would be christened tomorrow, with Brother Elias performing the rite in their cottage.

Finally, she saw Godwin. He was approaching the last small rise south of Bordweal, Saedraca loping easily beneath him. The stallion's powerful muscles swelled under a glistening black coat as he dug mighty hooves into the sod. A little way behind rode Bosa and Eilaf, and beyond them, riding at an unhurried pace, came another. At first, Constance did not recognize this unexpected rider, though something in his lean, languid posture struck her as familiar. As they drew nearer, she saw that it was Fulk de Oilly, the archbishop's man. Then she recalled Godwin telling her he would be the chief justice at the faircourt.

Constance stood to smooth her garment. She had taken

extra care in dressing, selecting a pale violet gown. Cynwyse said the color lit her honey hair, made her blue eyes seem periwinkle. She watched as Godwin suddenly checked Saedraca to lean from the horse and retrieve something. Curious, she put a hand to her brow and squinted into the distance, smiling when she saw it was Cuthbert. Earlier, the terrier had heard Godwin's name mentioned and went immediately to take up watch in the south field. All morning he waited, hardly visible in the grass, a small gray sentinel with wiry fur gazing toward Hexham. The party disappeared from view as it headed toward the stable.

Tom traded pipes for fiddle and began plucking out a carol-dance. Folk stopped their visiting to enthusiastically clap in time, and a circle of dancers soon formed, arms linked. Tom and Matilda took up positions in the center. As the song ended, several shouted the names of other favorites. One seemed to catch Tom's fancy, for his eyes danced and his bow went happily home. A lively tune sprang forth. He was accompanied by Matilda, who, clapping and skipping, brayed out the lyrics. The dancers took several steps to the right as she sang of a young girl's seduction by a Scotsman. The crowd then marked time treading left, bellowing out the chorus—"And she was the Flower of Northumberland!"

Matilda was crooning, "The young maid's love was easily won" as Godwin and Fulk strode up the lane with Cuthbert tucked under Godwin's arm. As customary, his garb was informal, dark chestnut hair tousled. But draped across his shoulders was a finely spun cape dyed rich green. Fulk, always the bandy rooster, wore hose and a knee-length tunic fastened with a glittering belt. He, too, wore a fine cloak, held by a red brooch. Small and well built, Fulk's dark looks were enhanced by vivid eyes that could shine with merriment or glaze over with boredom.

Godwin greeted Constance with a smile, putting Cuthbert down to clasp both her hands. "You look lovely, Constance."

"Indeed," Fulk chimed in, "like a beautiful woodland

enchantress from a bard's tale."

Constance laughed. "The fairy queen? I've read of her and she does not chase after a babe and oversee housework! But thank you, Fulk. An unexpected pleasure it is to have you at Bordweal."

"I fear I invited myself, lady, when I learned of our bailiff's plans." He shot Godwin an amused glance that suggested this was a simplified version of a more involved exchange. Godwin ignored him as he waved to several of the dancers who were shouting their greetings to the bailiff. He said, "A local favorite, this song!" Matilda was now singing plaintively of the poor maid's desertion at the border by the outlaw who had promised her everything.

Constance loved the music of Northumbria. She hired any passing minstrel, listening eagerly to the often haunting tunes. She would hear a poignant melody, sure the plaintive music expressed a tragic love affair or epic battle lost, only to find the lyrics quite silly, celebrating a black cow, the moon, or some such thing.

Bosa and Eilaf arrived from stabling the horses smelling of hay and livestock. Bosa's eyes grew large when he rounded the corner and saw the dancers. He stopped in his large tracks to stare, prompting Eilaf to fetch him forward. Everyone knew that Bosa loved to dance. Tom began another reel and newcomers joined in. Bosa loped to the circle while others stepped away to catch their breath. Eilaf pulled a face at the very notion of dancing.

The melody was light and fanciful, and therefore Constance expected it to describe a tragedy. Matilda cartwheeled around the ring several times before singing out, "Giants and fairies throng the brooks, the whole green earth is fairyland!" The dancers hooted wildly, and Constance guessed this was another local favorite. Godwin held a hand out to her, a smile on his lips, "Will you dance with me, lady?"

"Nay! I cannot carol-dance."

"But it's easy!" he assured her. "Come, let me show you."

She took his hand as Matilda sang, "You find them in dim woodland nooks!" Then the chorus shouted, "Giants and fairies throng the brooks!" But Constance hung back, undecided. She knew it would not be proper to dance among her tenants. Godwin often cared not about propriety, but oughtn't she?

Fulk was lounging on the bench, watching them with amusement. "Godwin, you oaf. Her Norman breeding's too fine for you!" Godwin, ignoring him, smiled broadly at Constance, tugging her hand. Then Aldwin saw his uncle and made a dash for his legs, squealing with pleasure. Constance thought she was spared, but Godwin simply scooped up Aldwin in one arm and pulled her forward with the other. Why not, she thought, and together they joined the others in the circle as Matilda sang, "They hide within the harvest stooks, and where the spotted foxgloves stand!" The ring of dancers opened for Godwin and Constance. They all skipped in time to the left, shouting, "Giants and fairies throng the brooks, the whole green earth is fairyland!"

Fulk said irritably, "Fetch me some wine, boy!" and Eilaf obligingly scurried off. He looked at the dog. "It's just you and me, then." Cuthbert growled deep in his throat.

Long after the feast was over and the bonfire had been lit, yet with plenty of light remaining in the evening sky, Godwin suggested to Constance they take a ride to the hermitage. Bosa and Eilaf were elected to accompany them, and Fulk decided that he too needed a ride after such a *grand* feast. Constance heard the sarcasm in his voice and let some creep into her own when she said, "I'm sure we were honored by your presence at our modest gathering, Fulk."

He replied that no gathering was humble if it included her, and was expanding on this theme when she smiled blandly and turned away, following Godwin to the stable.

When the horses were saddled, they set out. Bosa and Eilaf rode as eager vanguard, keen to give rein to their mounts, while Constance and Godwin followed at a more leisurely pace. Fulk played the bored rearguard.

A tiny cottage, the hermitage sits nestled deep in priory woodland, just east of Bordweal's wide pastures. It had been constructed to serve those canons who occasionally desired to withdraw from the bustle of town life, as a temporary refuge where a man of God could reach out to the holy through prayer, solitude, and abstinence. In reality, it was a hunting lodge.

Though acting prior Brother Elias had expressly forbid it, many of the canons still hunted in the forests of the priory, often with local knights and gentry. The hermitage provided handy, if rustic, quarters in the thick of the forest. Constance thought the canons' behavior deplorable and suggested as much to Godwin once, but he only smiled, saying it was harmless. On occasion, the remote hermitage also proved appealing to outlaws, and she knew Godwin inspected it frequently.

They talked of many things as they rode, letting their conversation meander from topic to topic. The bell for Vespers was ringing as they entered the forest, traveling along a welltrodden path. The oak and hazel trees were old and vast, their leafy tops suppressing the nuisance of tangled undergrowth present in younger woodland. Small colonies of fern and holly were all that grew within the shadowy interior. A clearing opened and there stood the hermitage. Godwin asked Constance to remain behind with Fulk while he had a look. Then he, Bosa, and Eilaf tied their mounts to a gnarled stump and approached the cottage.

"We may as well stretch our legs, too," Fulk suggested, nimbly dismounting to come over and assist Constance. He held her longer than was necessary, smiling at her disapproval. "There is a reason I came today," he said.

"Oh?" Constance looked beyond Fulk to see Godwin approaching the cottage. His back stiffened and he drew his sword, holding up the other hand, signaling for Bosa and Eilaf to stay back. He opened the door and stepped through. She said, "Fulk, I think something is amiss."

He glanced over his shoulder, unconcerned. "Godwin has matters well in hand. And you are safe with me."

"Am I?" she replied archly, glaring at him before returning her gaze to the hermitage. She gave a sigh of relief when Godwin reappeared in the doorway, motioning to Bosa and Eilaf.

"Oh yes. I feel a great fondness for you, Lady Constance. I would never allow harm to *touch* you," he said. He reached for her hand and she stepped back to avoid him, but regretted the impulse, for he looked at her with a curious, rather wounded, expression. She was overreacting. He was only being courteous.

"You may not share my affections, Constance, but perhaps in time you'll grow to care for me. Who can say?" He shrugged. "It's an added boon, don't you think, when a couple united in marriage share true love?" He took a step toward her, eyes roaming over her face.

Constance did not back away. She had learned that Fulk thrived on cat and mouse games, and she was determined not be his mouse. "I feel toward you as I would any acquaintance, Fulk. As for the intimacy of marriage, I consider it inappropriate for you and I to discuss."

He laughed softly at her prim speech. "Oh, but it is appropriate," he countered.

Constance gave him a puzzled stare and then looked past his shoulder to see Godwin emerge from the cottage. "Forgive me, I rather got ahead of myself," Fulk explained. "You see, I've been thinking it's time I take a wife, and the archbishop is eager to reward my loyal service by granting me the lady of my choice. And I chose you."

Godwin came over to join them, oblivious to the knot of tension. "Someone's been staying in the hermitage. I thought at first it might be an outlaw—the lock is gone," he said. "But nothing else is amiss. I suspect it was a careless canon. Constance, what's wrong?"

"Your timing is the worst, Godwin, as always," Fulk said, his eyes never leaving Constance. "But I suppose you may as well hear this. It concerns you, too." He smiled slyly. "I was just explaining to the lady that the archbishop has granted my wish. Constance and I are to be married."

Six ✝

K ing Arthur and his knights came swiftly to the forest. On a
Spanish hunter, the king led the chase, flushing the white
stag from its hiding place. The baying hounds pursued it while
the archers' arrows flew thick and fast.

In the midst of the hunt, Yves was seized by a desire to seek
his own adventure. In the woods he followed a path, a very difficult trail full of briars and thorns. With great hardship he
made his way, riding the whole day before finally coming to
open country. At the edge of the plain stood a cliff with a steep
bank overlooking a bay. There was a solitary ship in the harbor,
fit and ready to launch. Its sail was woven silk, the deck solid
ebony.

Yves went down to the harbor expecting to find men guarding
the priceless vessel. Instead, he found only a giant hind, which
immediately challenged him to battle. Yves swiftly took his bow
and shot it, striking the beast in the breastbone. She fell at once,
but the arrow rebounded, giving him a dreadful wound. The
arrow had gone through his thigh and into the horse's flank,
forcing Yves to dismount. He collapsed on the thick grass beside
the hind.

The wounded animal groaned loudly with her pain. Then she

spoke, saying, "Alas! I am dying! And you, vassal, who wounded me, this shall be your destiny: may you never find a remedy for your wound! Neither herb nor root, neither healer nor potion will cure you of that injury, until a woman restores you, one who will suffer, out of love for you, pain and grief such as no woman ever suffered before. And out of love for her, you will suffer as much. Now go and leave me in peace."

Badly wounded, Yves made his shirt into a bandage, tightly binding his bleeding thigh. He then boarded the ship to seek aid, but found no one. Amidships he discovered a bed of cypress and ivory with a silken coverlet. Exhausted, he lay down. When he awoke, he tried to leave the vessel, but discovered it had set sail! It was on the high seas, carrying him swiftly away. Still weary, he returned to the bed and fell fast asleep. . . .

SEVEN ✚

Master Gruffydd was in a state; he had much to do and little time. There were his booth and wares to see to, final matters concerning the guild feast—a host of tasks requiring his direct supervision—yet all he could think about was Maegden. He pushed away the bread and cheese, willing himself to rise from the table, to don his cape and command the day. But will as he might, he remained slumped on the bench.

As a rule, he could do that—will things to happen, take control of a situation and shape it to his liking. When he wanted something, his mind formed a list of objectives, the means to a desired end. Then he completed each, one by one, until he had what he wanted. That was how he acquired his wife.

She was the younger daughter of a local nobleman. He snorted, pondering his in-laws. They were noble according to some rusty sword they kept locked away in a trunk and a scrap of parchment—likely forged—that recorded their lineage and past deeds. They were also poor as pauper soup. Gruffydd, on the other hand, was rich. He owned a house in town, large and well appointed, wore fine clothes and gave generously to the poor. But he was humble, would always be humble.

The first moment he saw Maegden, he wanted her. But

many other suitors had lined up to claim her, for she was beautiful *and* noble. Many could overlook her poverty, himself included. Gruffydd's strategy, however, was superior to his rivals. He courted the father, not Maegden, granting him a generous loan at very low interest over a period of several years. The money was used to buy back a portion of the family's land to endow the only son. Gruffydd also sold him goods at a discount, bought the man's wool for more than its worth and gave generously to the convent founded in the family's name. Maegden was not pleased with the outcome of this courtship, but submitted without protest as a woman ought.

At first, their marriage was a paradise. He showered her with fine clothing and trinkets, hired servants to wait on her, listened patiently to her prattling. She in turn yielded to the unexpected passions of his meager loins. Their lovemaking was exquisite, and he reveled in her night after night, mornings too, although he was committing the sin of lust. But he could not help himself, nor did she mind his insatiable desire, always surrendering herself at his first fumbling touch. She was docile and willing, as a wife should be, a combination that excited him to peaks of pleasure he could barely withstand. And he was gentle, so gentle with his doll-like Maegden.

But something had gone terribly wrong, for she had grown cold and distant. At first he thought she was with child and forgave her every sullen word, her rigid stillness when he groped for her in the night. But a month went by, then two with no signs of a babe. Finally, he asked what ailed her. Was she angry? No, Maegden assured him, she only missed her family. So he arranged a stay with her parents, and when she returned, she was pleasanter, but still withdrawn.

He was patient as could be, did not push, or pry. Their coupling resumed, but he sensed a change. She submitted without complaint, as before, but sometimes, he saw looks of loathing cross her face as he fondled her, felt her stiff revulsion as he mounted her young body. Maegden's disgust did not dampen his ardor, of course, for a good woman naturally feels this way about her wifely duty, but he wondered at the change. What brought it on?

Then, it finally happened, Gruffydd got her with child! He was overjoyed, relieved, and for the first time in their short marriage, felt as if he truly possessed his wife. But his happiness was short-lived. . . .

What could be wrong? She had wealth, everything she could want. Why was she not happy? He wanted her to be content as before, but for once in his life, he could not think what to do.

Wearily, he pushed himself from the table. The smell of cheese was making his tender stomach queasy. Maegden had already left, gone to help Hafren manage her brood. She was spending more and more time with her sister, drawn to the children no doubt. His dimpled face flushed, thinking of his own failure.

Gruffydd retrieved his cloak from its peg. The servants had gone as well, for it was customary to give hired help a holiday on opening day, a tradition he approved. He was a fair master, understanding that evenhanded treatment was the key to managing servants. Beatings should be rare, the mere threat of a thrashing enough to inspire dedicated service. Yet, when required, a thorough job should be made of it to produce a lasting impression.

Like a magnet, these thoughts drew him back to Maegden, for he approached marriage in much the same way. He was kind, indulgent even, disciplining only when necessary. In return his wife was cold and willful. How just was this? With a sigh, he went into the street.

It was quiet near the Market Square where Gruffydd's stone house sat solidly between the priory cathedral and the bailiff's Moot Hall. It was fitting that his home should occupy the very heart of Hexham. Normally, the square buzzed with activity, market day or no, for it was the town's main crossroad. Now, however, the square and nearby streets were depressingly deserted, reflecting his dreary mood.

While the fair was in session on the haugh, all selling and trading was prohibited in town. Tradesmen and merchants rented booths like outsiders if they wanted to peddle goods. They could turn their shops into boarding houses, though, which is what most folk did. At the moment, no boarders walked the streets, for it seemed everyone was at the fair.

He turned down Gilesgate, thinking he had better get there, too. Assistants were operating his stalls, and he did not trust them. Pilfering was a constant worry. He paid his workers fairly, like his house servants, but a generous salary was no guarantee of honesty. When presented with enviable items and the opportunity to nick them, no one among the humble could resist, and Gruffydd kept a meticulous inventory of his goods.

Though it was still early, the sun was warm, promising a hot day. Already Gruffydd was sweating freely under his cloak and by the time he passed the locked gates of the priory, a heavy, pungent odor was wafting from his flapping cape. But he was not thinking of the heat, nor the arduous walk or his own ripe smell. He was again contemplating Maegden. Was *she* honest? A horrid little thought had been needling the darkest recesses of his mind, an idea so hideous he wouldn't let it surface. No! He shook his head at the notion.

"Hoy, Master Gruffydd," a voice called. He turned to see Fara, Hexham's herbalist and healer, coming down the sloping street at her usual brisk pace. He stopped to wait, waving a listless hand, too winded and distraught to utter a greeting. There were only a few residents of Hexham whom Gruffydd truly respected, and Fara was among them. Her origins were lowlier than his, her father a leper, her mother a healer who had abandoned both husband and daughter when Fara was only a child. But she, like Gruffydd, had overcome the life bestowed at birth to become a respected member of the community. She was also lovely—not round and enticing like his Maegden, but gravely serene, like a carved image of the Virgin.

"On your way to the fair, are you?" he asked as she drew up next to him, looking fresh as dew and smelling of lavender.

"Aye, and later than I'd like. But I've had a sick child to tend."

"Not Gwynn I hope."

"Nay, a neighbor." They resumed their walking, she keeping pace with his slow gait. She was like that always, he thought, attentive and considerate. When his irritable stomach forced him to bed, as it was wont to do, she was never repulsed by his bloated condition, but ministered with gentle care. Maegden had once been that way, or so he liked to remember.

"Are you well, Master Gruffydd? Is your stomach troubling you this morning?"

He belched discretely, tasting rancid cheese. Nodding to her, he swallowed down the bitter bile. "Whatever I eat disagrees," he complained.

"And the mugwort does no good?"

"Some," he said, not wanting to impugn her remedy.

"Perhaps you should consult the leech. He is quite learned, I hear. He may have a better remedy."

"Surely not," Gruffydd objected with some heat. "You are as learned as any man of university."

Fara smiled. "Always there is more to learn, Master Gruffydd, and we should take advantage of his presence. You should consult the leech."

"As you wish," he said, adding, "He is gifted with the sight, or so people are chattering."

Fara said nothing. Gruffydd knew she did not abide spells and fortune telling, but he was suddenly struck by an idea. He quickened his pace, wanting now to see the leech as quickly as possible.

Gruffydd was disappointed when they reached the fair site. Of course, it was swarming with every resident of the shire, as he knew it would be, along with the many outsiders who had traveled far to attend the annual event. But the leech's booth was exceptionally popular, and a long line wended from its lone, solemn occupant. With a sigh, he took up a position at the rear, forgetting his own booth. Fara said she would return later, when the wait wasn't so long. Gruffydd barely heard her words, and she left him as he was impatiently counting the number of people between himself and the healer.

Craning his neck, Gruffydd tried to get a look at the man who might provide him with answers. This was what he desperately needed, he realized with a clarity he had not possessed for months. He could not begin to address the problem with his wife until he understood the source of her misery. This required that he first confront his mounting suspicions, and surely, a skilled leech knew many ways to divine the truth. Once Gruffydd learned this truth, he could take steps to right the matter. And they might be drastic ones, indeed, if his fears proved correct.

As he drew closer to the head of the line, Gruffydd could more easily study the man and his collection of goods. He appeared competent, a bit undernourished, but sound. His eyes were vague, but his manner attentive. The booth was stocked with every imaginable herb—dried and fresh—an array of flowers, several large, well-used books, and some metal instruments that made Gruffydd shudder as he imagined their function. There was also a small hearth where water boiled in a copper pot, a vent to let out smoke, and jars of substances stacked all around. Shutters could be drawn to close off the booth, presumably for procedures requiring privacy.

Gruffydd could also hear more clearly the ailments being described by those in line ahead of him: aching joints, ailing livestock, harelips, poisonous in-laws, bleeding gums, cursed fields, evil lumps beneath the skin, elf-shot. . . . On and on it went. After hearing a complaint, the leech would often thumb through one of his books to derive a cure. He then mixed a concoction by infusing herbs into boiling water, sometimes adding honey, oil, or a curious dark substance, often chanting in a strange tongue as he prepared the tonic. Other times, he blended a salve using butter with various ingredients. He gave clear instructions with each remedy, emphasizing the importance of adhering to them. Prayers, chants, and incantations he wrote out carefully on scraps of cloth. Most could not read, of course, but they had only to wave the words over the brew to ensure its success. On occasion, an infliction was too serious for on-the-spot treatment, as with the man with nose polyps, and appointments were made for more extreme procedures.

The sun was high overhead as Gruffydd drew to the front of the line. The man just ahead was complaining of a sty on his eye. Without even opening a book, the leech retrieved a brass vessel, pouring from it a dark liquid that obviously contained garlic and onions. Into a clay vial the pungent mixture went. Handing it to the man, the leech instructed him to apply a small amount every evening using a feather. The relieved patient handed over his money, and then it was Gruffydd's turn.

Stepping up to the stall, he was suddenly nervous, realizing that many would overhear his conversation, just as he had avidly attended others. Several of the dratted canons were just behind him, with Brother John practically stepping on his cape. He could not speak openly to the leech, for news of his "malady" would spread in no time. He would become an object of scorn and derision—an intolerable prospect. Besides, now that the moment was here, Gruffydd wondered if he truly wanted an answer to his query. His stomach heaved painfully at the thought, sending up a fiery ball of festering cheese.

He stood rooted at the counter, staring stupidly at the leech, clutching his exploding midsection. Up close, the healer's eyes were large and gray. When focused, as they were now on Gruffydd, they appeared wise and intelligent. Surely, he could trust this man. The leech waited patiently while Brother John nudged him. "Go on then! Out with it!" the canon said. "There's a pack of us back here, Master Gruffydd, and we'd like to have our turn *today!*"

"My stomach," Gruffydd finally managed, his voice peeping like a newly hatched wren. "It burns with food. Mugwort does no good."

The leech nodded his understanding, then turned to prepare a remedy. Retrieving a large bunch of purplish stalks with parsley-like leaves and round airy seed heads, he peeled off several and handed them to his patient saying, "This is the healing plant of the archangel St. Michael. It is an excellent cure for ailments such as yours. Chop a handful of leaves and roots and boil them in water for a tea. Drink one cup before every meal."

Mutely, Gruffydd took the bundle of leafy stalks. They were very fragrant, like honey. The leech told him his price and added that if the archangel's herb proved successful, he would inform Gruffydd how to grow the plant himself. Could he return tomorrow? Gruffydd nodded, knowing he would never come back. He fumbled in his purse for the coins. As he put them in the outstretched hand of the leech, he opened his mouth to speak. He wanted to say he had another, more serious complaint, but no words came.

Brother John snorted impatiently and Gruffydd decided to leave. He was just turning away when the leech held up a hand to silence the brother's churning haste and motioned for Gruffydd to come inside the booth through the side entrance. He serenely drew the shutters, peremptorily cutting off the objections of the canon, saying, "A moment, please."

Gruffydd's face burned. What must people think? A private consultation with the leech was sure to generate all manner of rumor! The leech, knowing he had something else to say, waited for him to speak. Gruffydd thought he might as well—folk be damned, let them think what they wanted! No wild rumor could be worse than the truth, if what he suspected was true. He squared his shoulders, but kept his voice at a low whisper when he said, "I fear my wife is unfaithful, that she has a lover. I understand you have the sight. Can you confirm or deny my fears?"

The leech's expression did not change. To Gruffydd's relief, no look of contempt, pity, or amusement crossed the grave countenance. "A serious matter," he said. "I understand your reluctance to speak. I can help you, yes, but not by these hands." He held them out for both to inspect. They were stained and leathery, the fingers long and tapering. "They are for healing, not divination." At Gruffydd's crestfallen face, he assured him, "But I know of several ways to test the faithfulness of a wife. I can also show you ways to ensure the honesty of a business partner or the celibacy of a priest. Yet these methods are indications only, not proof."

"Yes, yes, I understand," Gruffydd said. "What must I do?"

The leech went over to a crockery jar filled with an assortment of fragrant flowers. Selecting two—a yellow lily and a white rose—he handed them to Gruffydd, saying, "Offer her a choice. If she selects the rose, her heart is pure. If her choice falls to the lily, she is false."

Grasping his flowers and herb stalks, Gruffydd stumbled from the booth without a backward glance. The leech stared after him, a smile playing at the lips, then he reopened the shutters to hear a canon complain of a failing libido.

Gruffydd hastened to his own booth. He was selling from two, one dealing in wool, the other specialty goods. The latter was closest—wedged along Haugh Lane between a furrier and a dealer of wax. His was artfully heaped with imports of Eastern silks, luxury cloths, spices, perfumes, dyestuffs, and jewelry. But he paid no notice to the display, or to the customers studying his wares, or the stammering assistants shocked by his late arrival. He waved them away as he frantically hunted for something to hold his precious flowers. Finding a jar, he ordered one to fetch water so his plucked beauties could be kept fresh. They must appear delightful, and substitutes would not do, he reasoned, for these were the flowers of the *leech*. Surely, they had magical properties. His assistants stared at one another, open-mouthed, and then hustled from the stall, convinced their master had gone mad.

EIGHT✦

The white Arabian mare galloped madly across the fields of Bordweal. Brother Elias clung desperately to her mane, black habit billowing, sandaled feet beating the air as he bobbed wildly in the saddle. He tried once more to rein in the beast, but his efforts went unheeded. She was swifter than the wild roe's startled flight and as untamed as her desert origins. He sent up a fervent prayer to Jude, patron saint of desperate situations.

In the distance, he saw a knot of people gathered near the manor house, mounted on steeds as if preparing to depart. Brother Elias dared lifting his arm to throw out a frantic wave, trying to communicate his peril. The risk proved unnecessary, however, for the mare suddenly swerved in her tracks, making straight for the startled onlookers. As she cantered fiercely on, drawing him closer, Brother Elias saw wonderment and alarm on the staring faces.

She came to an abrupt halt near the steward's horse. The mare then dipped her great head and danced several paces closer to the stallion in a manner that was both frolicsome and demur. Brother Elias leapt from her back to gaze shakily up at the people gathered around. There was Lady Constance, elegantly clad, her eyes concerned. Astride a sturdy old cob was the cook, Cynwyse, clucking her tongue. Hereberht, sitting straight as truth in the saddle, wore his usual affronted expression as he gazed down his nose at the disheveled monk. Two squires smirked from their ponies.

Lady Constance quickly climbed from her palfrey to put a steadying hand on his arm. "Brother Elias, are you all right?" Stunned, he could only nod a reply, and she turned her gaze to the mare. "Is this *your* beast?"

He stammered, feeling his face go red. "It is . . . rather it belongs to the priory—a gift from a crusader. She was yearning for exercise . . . and, as I had to come here for the baptism, I thought to give the poor thing a stretch. . . ." His voice trailed off. He sounded absurd, even to his own ears. Worse, he realized he was not being truthful. He had been captivated by the horse from the moment the knight led her into the priory precinct, eager to fly with the proud Arab. He cast his eyes upon the ground, too ashamed to say more.

Constance said, "She is a generous gift, indeed. You are wise to take extra care with such a proud mount, brother. They'll not endure long days of confinement." She stroked its mane, singing softly, "White as the wild swan's plumage bright."

"She *is* beautiful, is she not?" Brother Elias said, perking up. "So pure . . . like a heavenly messenger. . . ."

"Aye, that may be so, brother," Cynwyse said. "But her needs are earthly, if ye take my meaning." The cook motioned with her gray head to the stallion. His dark eyes were bulging as he pranced near the mare. Hereberht jerked the reins once, bringing him to a restless halt, but not before he reared back to loudly snort an objection.

Brother Elias furrowed his brow, looking from mare to stallion. Comprehension dawned. "Oh," he said faintly, blushing again.

Cynwyse chuckled. "You oughtn't ride the mare when she's in heat, brother. There's no telling where she might take ye to slake her thirst! The boys grinned at each other, and Constance hastened to say, "You may stable her at Bordweal, if you wish, brother, while you administer the baptism. We're leaving for the fair. Once we have gone, she will no doubt quiet down."

"Thank you, lady." He reached a slender white arm for the reins, holding them tentatively.

"You must be more firm with the animal," Hereberht chided.

"She's really quite mild," he assured the steward. Then, turning to Constance, he said, "Don't let me keep you. You must be keen to reach the fair."

They said farewell, Constance adding that she looked forward to seeing him at the guild feast that evening. "Oh yes, the feast," Brother Elias answered vaguely, "I'd almost forgotten. . . ."

She smiled faintly as she remounted, wondering again whether Brother Elias was a suitable prior for St. Andrews. She adored him, of course—who did not? He was earnest and caring, yet these were not necessarily desirable in a prior, whose responsibilities were demanding. He must be capable of managing his house while maintaining order and discipline among the canons. In the case of St. Andrews, a rather impoverished priory filled with unruly brothers, it would be a challenging task for any candidate, and perhaps outright harmful to one so gentle as Brother Elias.

As they got underway, Constance thought how steeped he was in his calling, a man of true faith. On the other hand, she sensed mettle beneath his delicate exterior, and he was exceptionally intelligent. There may be more to Brother Elias than meets the eye. . . .

They started down the familiar trail to the river. From this vantage point, one could see the fair site with its array of booths and tents stretched along the haugh. Already a great many people were gathered. At the center of it all stood the justice's pavilion. As her gaze fixed upon the large tent, Constance's thoughts were pulled back to Fulk, where they had mostly dwelled since the previous evening. She would never marry him, of course. The idea was absurd.

Goaded by thoughts of his audacious proposal, she urged her horse to a canter, and then just as suddenly checked its pace. Fulk would find her discomfort amusing, she thought, and vowed to put him from her mind. Besides, there really was no cause for concern. He could not force a marriage, however powerful his lord; her consent was required. Fulk was baiting her was all, and her own lord and father-in-law, Eilan, would never agree to the marriage. She could count on his support, and his was a powerful voice in the north.

Constance reined in the horse to give Cynwyse time to come alongside her. Hereberht and the squires, Giles and Tilly, hung back a bit, yet kept a close watch over their mistress. The cook was occupied with her prayers. She did not enjoy outings on horseback and passed the time with appeals to the Almighty—not directly to *Him*, but to a hierarchical web of divine power. Constance had learned that there were particular saints whom she appealed for certain things: St. Christopher for a safe journey, St. Antony for a lost needle, St. Luke for a sore tooth. Serious matters were referred to St. Peter, while graver circumstances required the aid of the Virgin. Dire situations necessitated Christ's direct intervention. Constance had never known Cynwyse to pray directly to God. "He's a busy man, that one," she once explained. "What's more, it wouldn't be proper goin' straight to the top. Would ye seek the king if a neighbor stole a pot?"

She also prayed briskly. "They don't like dilly-dallying," she once explained. "Say what troubles ye and be done with it. Many folk have they to tend." Now she was calling on St. Peter. Curious, Constance waited to hear her petition, for she rarely troubled the keeper of the gates, though he was her favorite. "Peter," she said, "rid us of Fulk."

Constance burst out laughing. "All the saints in heaven couldn't do that I'm afraid, dear Cynwyse! Leastways, not before the fair's over. He's the archbishop's chief justice." She shook her head at the irony. "He directs the faircourt. Can you imagine? Why, I'm sure he doesn't know the meaning of the word *justice*!"

"'Tis'n't the faircourt I'm bothered about, lady. He's pegged ye for his wife. What will ye do?"

"I have refused his proposal. The matter is closed."

Cynwyse heaved a great sigh. "And ye thinks that snake of a man will leave it at that?"

"He can't *force* marriage on me. I have liberties through law, though I am a woman."

"Lady, ye must consider. He has powerful friends, that one, folk who *make* the law."

"Fulk will be an annoyance for a few days, but that's all. He'll soon tire of the hunt. Men like him do when their quarry give no chase."

" 'Tis a serious matter, lady," Cynwyse warned. "Ye ought to give it more thought."

"But what else is there to do but refuse?"

The cook snorted and rolled her eyes. "For one so learned, ye are daft as a post at times! Might it be that ye are promised to another?"

Constance stared at the cook. "You mean . . . be untruthful?"

"Nay! Ye and I both know there *is* another, though neither of ye have spoken of it. Mayhap it's time."

"No."

"And why not? 'Twould smartly end the matter with the scoundrel Fulk."

"Enough, Cynwyse," Constance warned. They were approaching the bridge, meeting up with more and more folk coming to the fair from the north. She looked back to see Hereberht and the squires close by, careful to let no one come between themselves and Constance.

The cook clucked her tongue but knew when to let a subject rest. Changing tack with a sigh, she said, " 'Twill have to be a charm then—something powerful." The party dismounted, and as they led the horses across the bridge, Cynwyse added, "Don't ye worry, lady. I'll find the right one."

It was as if they had traveled a long distance to a great city, so crowded with folk and sounds and smells was Hexham's fair. Constance laughed, forgetting Fulk, delighting instead in the day's prospects.

But Hereberht, face grim, was addressing her, and such was the clamor Constance couldn't hear his words. Moving closer, he told her he was eager to go about his own business for the manor, but was concerned about the size of the crowd. Would two squires be escort enough for his lady? Glancing at Giles and Tilly, his expression was doubtful. The reins of the horses were slack in their hands as they stared at the bustling crowd and nearby wares.

Hereberht's task at the fair was formidable: to procure the goods and supplies Bordweal would require in the coming year—everything from livestock to candle wax. Over the next week, he would negotiate with vendors, reach agreements on delivery dates and terms, and see to it that all transactions were properly drawn up in notarized contracts, a service provided by the faircourt.

"We'll be fine, Hereberht," Constance assured him. But still he hesitated. She repeated her words, a bit impatiently this time, and the steward's face cleared.

Constance was pleased, but then realized he was looking past her. She turned to see Godwin coming to meet them, and understood the steward's relief. Who better in Hexham to look after his mistress than the bailiff? Hereberht hadn't even been listening to her. But what did it matter? She was happy to see Godwin and her face betrayed as much as she greeted him.

"I've been watching for you," he said. "I was hoping to escort you and Cynwyse, if you are willing. I don't remember an opening day so busy!"

"We would be very pleased," Constance said. "But will we keep you from your duties?"

"Nay, I'd be strolling about either way. And I've got men posted everywhere. Come, what shall we inspect first, ladies—silks, furs, wines?"

Satisfied, Hereberht departed. Giles and Tilly were given the morning free once they had the horses stabled.

Constance asked them where they would go first. To see the hunting birds, of course, they exclaimed together. The boys were mesmerized of late by gyrfalcons, sparrow hawks, and goshawks, and their youthful excitement made her think of Aldwin. How delightful it will be, she thought, when he's old enough to come to the fair.

As it happened, the food stalls were closest. Like the steward, Cynwyse had long-range requirements to consider—the necessary quantities of grain, spices, dried fruit, nuts, salted fish, and meat. Hereberht did the actual purchasing, though, and about a week before the fair, the two met to prepare a supply list. A trying event, Constance had absented herself from the meeting, for they usually argued dreadfully. Though thrifty by nature, Cynwyse's demands could be extravagant when it came to her kitchen, contrary to the steward's frugal management philosophy. This year, however, their stubborn disagreements had been minimal, according to a triumphant Cynwyse, and Constance wondered if her steward wasn't mellowing.

Though she would not be making the larger purchases, Cynwyse loved prowling through the food stalls looking for new or unusual ingredients. She dwelled long at the spicers' booths and while she was occupied, Godwin led Constance away from the main thoroughfare to say, "I don't know what Fulk is up to, but you needn't be concerned. I plan to have a talk with him today. You can be sure I'll straighten him out." He looked at her carefully. "That is, if you'd like me to."

"Oh yes, I'd be very grateful, Godwin. I want nothing to do with the man. Honestly, I think he delights in tormenting folk."

"Yes, Fulk can be a devil," Godwin said. "But his . . . proposal is not exactly unusual or unexpected is it?" When he saw her look he hastened to add, "I'm not suggesting you encouraged him or that his methods are not wrong. But, Constance, did you not expect suitors?" he asked, adding in a low voice, "I think many have held back out of respect for your loss."

Cynwyse came over with several bundles, and they went next to sample wine. Constance ordered two barrels of Burgundy, one to be sent to Bordweal, the other to the guild feast. When they came to the leech's booth, Cynwyse was bitterly disappointed by the long queue, for she had been looking forward to discussing charms and potions with the reportedly learned man. "Ach, will ye look at the line!" she cried. "We'll not wait in this heat! We must come back when his popularity's waned a bit."

They continued down the row of booths flanking Haugh Lane, where specialty goods and rare imports tended to be concentrated. When Cynwyse was lured to a booth offering rabbit skins and lambskin trimmings, Constance asked Godwin, "Is there any news from Dunbar?"

He shook his head, and then took her hand, saying, "You shouldn't worry. It would take more than a stray arrow to bring down that tree!"

When Cynwyse rejoined them, Constance said, "There is Master Gruffydd's booth. I understand he has some fine miniver hoods. Shall we look?"

They came up to his stall just as Gruffydd's wife Maegden and her sister Hafren were approaching from the opposite direction, encircled by Hafren's daughters. The little ones rushed to the booth, captivated by the array of treasure spread out to entice buyers. As they greeted one another, Constance thought that Maegden looked pale, her manner strained.

Then Master Gruffydd bounded from his booth. He, too, looked pallid, his loud, ebullient greeting sounding hollow. Constance wondered if they were ill. She went with Cynwyse to view the hoods, but kept a surreptitious eye on the merchant, for he was behaving strangely—speaking overly loud, his limbs jerking like a puppet's. Godwin stood quietly by, and Constance sensed that he, too, was studying the couple. Hafren chased after the girls, keeping them from handling the costly wares.

"At last, my wife, you have come!" Gruffydd shouted. In

his hands he held a posy composed of two flowers and some greenery. Constance thought he was offering these to Maegden, but no, he put the herbs aside and held out the flowers to his wife, one in each hand. "Which pleases you the most?" he asked.

Maegden looked uncomfortable, as if her husband shamed her. She quickly took the yellow lily, hardly smiling in return. Gruffydd turned to Hafren who was pulling Hanna from the silks. He gave her the white rose, saying, "This falls to you, good sister-in-law."

Godwin was running late, and he had Master Gruffydd to thank. But he was sorry for the man, rather than annoyed. Earlier, as soon as he heard Maegden speak, he realized that it was she in the Moot Hall with Asheferth two nights ago.

Damn that knight! And where was he now? Not hunting, that was plain. Probably holed up somewhere nearby. But where?

As Gruffydd lumbered beside him, quaking with anger and clutching a weedy plant, Godwin wondered if the merchant knew the truth about his wife. Not likely, he thought, given the business with the flowers they had all witnessed. But if he did not know now, he soon would, for in a town as small as Hexham, secrets were hard to come by. He wondered what he ought to do—order Asheferth to break it off, or keep out of his knight's affairs.

They were on their way to the faircourt so that Gruffydd could make a complaint against a man who had apparently stiffed him. Today, an incident with the man happened late in the afternoon, after Constance returned to Bordweal. At his other booth, among the drapers and wool-mongers, Gruffydd had made a terrible scene. When the bailiff arrived with Wulfstan, the merchant's color was so high Godwin thought he must be having a fit. But no, according to Gruffydd, the accused had sold him a large quantity of wool at a negotiated price, and then reneged on the agreement.

The man refused the merchant his wool, leaving him short and unable to meet his commitments. Now he had come to the fair to sell the very wool he had promised Gruffydd!

Gruffydd was insisting that Godwin handle the matter, that he toss the "thief" in the Keep until the wrong had been made right, with interest! While his complaint, if true, was just cause for anger, something in the merchant's behavior—the shrillness of his accusation and his unbridled rage—worried Godwin, making him inclined to go along for now to ease the man's fury.

But he could not imprison the man—John Longspee was his name—for he vehemently denied the accusation. He maintained that it was Master Gruffydd who had tried to cheat *him*. Godwin allowed him to go on his way, once he produced a local to vouch for his name. The bailiff would question him later, if necessary, but it was clearly a matter for the faircourt. Gruffydd could barely contain his outrage, but agreed to go along with Godwin and lodge a complaint.

Inside the pavilion, they found two justices, but no Fulk. Godwin was annoyed, for he had planned to take him aside. That morning, he had noticed Fulk arriving late. Apparently he left early as well. How typical, Godwin thought, growing more annoyed. When he passed the tent earlier in the day, the chief justice had been sprawled on a bench, yawning and staring into the distance as a witness stood before him, recounting his story.

The justices were tired and irritable. They had already packed their gear and were preparing to depart for the day when Gruffydd arrived, and only Godwin's presence at his side moved them to hear the merchant's complaint. The scribe from St. Andrews had left already so that one of the justices had to pen the grievance. He let it be known that it was beneath his dignity. Gruffydd poured out his story, and with lips pursed, the justice recorded the words in a tight cursive script. The merchant was then hustled from the tent, assured that John Longspee would be duly summoned in the morning.

"I'll leave you now, Master Gruffydd," Godwin said once they were outside. "I have some other business." The fair site was almost deserted now, the last of the vendors closing up their stalls, his watchmen escorting stragglers from the grounds. Oddly, Gruffydd was no longer blustering, his mind far away as he clutched his stomach. "No doubt you've a thing or two to do yourself," Godwin added. "The guild feast is almost upon us. I'm sure it will be most memorable." He tried to sound encouraging for the despondent looking merchant. Was it business or his wife? With Gruffydd it could be either.

"I hope so, Lord Godwin," he answered. "Thank you for your assistance today," he added before wandering off in the direction of Gilesgate. Staring after him, Godwin was certain that he knew the truth about Maegden.

Nine✝

*T*he ship sailed a great distance to an ancient castle. The
stronghold was protected on one side by a great wall and by
the sea on the other. The lord who ruled here was an old man
with a young wife, a woman of good lineage, noble and beautiful. He was extremely jealous, and the watch he kept over her
was relentless. Inside the castle walls she resided in a guarded
chamber. A girl served her, a maid who was loyal and kind, and
there was great affection between the two women. No one else
came, man or woman, nor could the wife leave the walls of the
enclosure, except to walk along the seashore, for an old priest,
hoary with age, kept the gate key.

On that same day, the lady went to the seaside, taking her
maid. They saw a beautiful ship come sailing into the harbor,
but could see no one guiding it. The lady started to flee, but the
maid, who was wise and more courageous, comforted her, and
they went to investigate.

The maid boarded the ship, but found no living thing save the
sleeping knight. She saw how pale he was and thought him
dead, and quickly went back to her mistress. When she told her
what she had found, lamenting the dead man, the lady said,
"Let us go see him."

The lady entered the ship and went to the bed to stare at the knight, sadly contemplating his strength and beauty. She was filled with sorrow, and said it was a shame he had died so young. Putting her hand on his breast, she was surprised to find that it was warm and that a healthy heart beat beneath his ribs. The knight, who was only asleep, now woke up and saw her.

Yves was astonished and delighted by the sight of the lady, and when she asked him how he got there, what country he came from, he told her his tale from beginning to end. "I don't know where I have arrived! Beautiful one, I beg you, please advise me. I don't know where to go, and I cannot guide this ship."

She said, "My dear lord, I will be happy to instruct you. My name is Nicolette, and this is my husband's land. He is a rich man, but extremely old. He is also terribly jealous. On my word of honor, he keeps me locked in his stronghold. Yet if it pleases you to stay until you are better able to travel, my maid and I will accommodate you." Yves thanked Nicolette, saying he would stay with her. And so with difficulty they brought him secretly to the lady's chamber. . . .

TEN ✠

The guild feast was no mere banquet, but an evening-long event filled with an assortment of activities. It began with a Mass in honor of the fellowship's patron saint, St. Wilfrid, followed by a solemn procession from the cathedral to the Calefactory, where the guild's officers would light the great candles. The first barrel of ale would be opened so that members could "drink the guild." Next, prayers were said for brothers and sisters, both living and dead, and a collection taken for the poor. Finally, the entertainment would begin, accompanied by more ale and wine, followed by the feast.

No one could remember when the guild was first established—some claimed it was before the Normans. It thrived and languished through the years and had all but been abandoned when Gruffydd breathed new life into the fellowship by infusing it with his own wealth. Its precepts were simple: a voluntary association for mutual support and good works. Members in good standing could expect aid in times of need whether due to illness, theft, fire, or any disaster, including death.

They escorted their dead to the grave while the common purse assisted with burial costs and purchased prayers for the deceased. Members' pledges also maintained the hospital of St. Giles, a refuge for the sick and destitute. The guild had important patrons as well, local gentry who made generous contributions toward charitable enterprises, as when a poor section of town burned to the ground last year and had to be rebuilt. Benefactors were given places of honor at festive observances, their status properly acknowledged.

Lady Constance was one such patron, a position she had assumed as a widow. Now, as she stood in the nave of St. Andrews, she wondered where another of its patrons was. Next to her stood Eilaf and Godwin's mother, Gunnilda, and together they made up the front row of the guild congregation. Lord Acomb, another patron, who should have been among them, had sent his regrets, along with a minstrel and a generous quantity of venison for the feast. Fulk was not in attendance, to Constance's relief. Gunnilda was clearly annoyed by her son's tardiness, stretching her neck this way and that, paying no mind to Brother Elias's Mass.

Glancing over her shoulder, Constance was impressed by the number of people gathered in the cathedral. Immediately behind her stood the guild's knights and gentry, while beyond these came Gruffydd and his officers—merchants all. Next, stood the remainder of the fellowship, ranked according to status, determined by the amount of dues they paid. The association was indeed flourishing, she reflected, an inspiring demonstration of good will. Then she noticed how the knights held their heads high, faces aloof, how the well-to-do merchants formed a stalwart phalanx before the less wealthy. At the back stood the poor. They were given an open invitation to all guild events, so long as they observed their place in the hierarchy.

Yet despite the impressive number of guild folk in attendance, the huge nave was over half empty. Splendid was Wilfrid's gift to Hexham, a soaring cathedral that could accommodate hundreds. From his pulpit before the choir, Brother Elias's words resonated through the immensity of smooth stone like the voice of God. Clusters of pillars both huge and slender held up high arches of stone rendered delicate through softly pointed curves and deeply set openings.

Brother Elias was now reading a story of miraculous healing from St. Wilfrid's *vita*. His feast day was in October and Constance had found it bewildering that his day was celebrated in August, but she came upon many puzzling practices in the north and was growing used to the local customs.

Little of Wilfrid's original church now remained, for five hundred years had passed since he carried the precious relics of St. Andrew from Rome to sanctify his new northern minster. In the interval, many enemies had descended upon Hexham—Norsemen, Scots, Normans—coming like locusts to sack and raid by fire and sword. The church bore heavy wounds and was nearly destroyed, until the Austin canons came and undertook to nurture her back to the grandeur of Wilfrid's triumph. This was their patron's true bequest, a daring framework of greatness to be made whole again by his disciples.

As her eyes roved the vast interior, coming to rest upon Hexham's current crop of canons slumbering peacefully in the choir, Constance thought it unlikely that they would contribute much to the never-ending restoration of the priory cathedral; their aspirations were rooted in comfort, food and drink, and it was fortunate that their predecessors had been productive. Brother Elias was the exception, of course, a wise innocent among the worldly.

He was far away now, at the high altar, a vague shape amid clouds of incense. The canons roused themselves sufficiently to sing the Offertory so that Constance knew the bread and wine had been presented. Godwin slipped in just as the congregation was saying the Pater Noster. Gunnilda scowled as he wedged between them and leaned over to kiss his mother's parchment cheek. She brightened instantly and tucked an arm in his, easily mollified.

Now two of the canons retrieved the priory's most precious relic from its chapel shrine—the arm of St. Wilfrid encased in a gold reliquary fashioned to look like a human arm, but twice normal size. The canons formed the head of a procession that carried the relic to the south transept and out of the cathedral to the Calefactory. As the congregation followed, Constance felt vaguely pagan in her actions, gravely following the golden arm raised high.

Once in the Calefactory, Gruffydd and his officers took command of the proceedings by lighting the candles and opening the ale. Constance, Godwin and Gunnilda took their places at a table set upon a raised platform while the rest of the guild members took seats, once again according to their status. Tables and benches were arranged from high, or dais, to low end of the lengthy hall. The guild worthies and their families were situated in the middle of the room, below the gentry, knights, and canons.

Gunnilda situated herself between Constance and her son, and Godwin, looking vexed by the arrangement, instructed Eilaf to sit on Constance's other side. As the ale made its way around the hall, Gunnilda chided Godwin. "Son, you are dressed for hawking! Do you even *look* at the fine clothes I bring? And why were you late to Mass? It sets a bad example, you know—"

"At least your son attended, lady, which is more than I can say for myself, I am ashamed to admit." They all turned to see Fulk standing behind them. He had come through a door immediately behind the dais, which connected the Calefactory to the vestibule of the Chapter House. Smiling broadly, he took a place next to Eilaf just as Master Gruffydd stood and raised his cup to the guild. The membership and patrons did likewise and as they all drank, Constance saw Fulk watching her over the rim of his vessel, eyes bright with pleasure.

When it was time for the entertainment, Gruffydd stood once more to announce a drama in which performers would recreate a memorable event from the life of St. Wilfrid. The guild membership murmured their excitement, for many had never seen a play. Next to her, Eilaf whispered, "Bosa is a performer. He wanted me to have a part, too, but I wouldn't."

"Why not?" Constance asked.

He shrugged and made a face. But Constance thought he looked regretful as he eagerly watched the stage for signs of activity.

More ale and wine were sent around as the canons prepared to put on their drama. A narrow platform had been erected on the east side of the hall. Wooden folding screens were placed to hide the players and their props. Brother Elias stood to one side of these and began reading from a book, face red, voice quavering. *"On the crossing back from Gaul, Bishop Wilfrid's party in mid-sea was alarmed by a sudden violent storm and contrary winds, just like the disciples on the Sea of Galilee."*

The screens were pulled aside by Brothers Paul and Thomas to reveal five canons seated in a skiff held fast to the stage by a wooden brace. They began tossing themselves about wildly, bumping into one another and feigning wails of fear. Brother Paul and Brother Thomas now held a blue cloth low in front of the boat. They flapped it vigorously to mimic a churning sea. *"The wind howled, thunder clapped, and white-crested waves drove them toward the land of the South Saxons,"* Brother Elias ominously intoned, warming to his role now. From outside the hall came sounds of thunder. Constance guessed it was made by rolling casks of stones.

Her eyes moved to the audience. Folk were staring wide-eyed at the players, their faces rapt in the dimly lit room. Only Master Gruffydd's was twisted with pain as he held one hand to his stomach as the other reached for a cup.

"The waves left both men and ship high and dry. Forthwith, a great horde of pagans approached, intending to seize the vessel, carry off the captives, and slay those who resisted!" A horde of canons, led by Bosa, appeared in the doorway of the Calefactory. They stampeded on stage, shouting and brandishing wooden spears. With painted faces, the pagans leered and gnashed their teeth at the trembling, shipwrecked monks. *"Our holy bishop Wilfrid, anxious to save his companions, tried to pacify them with soothing words and*

promised them a large sum of money." Brother John leapt from the boat, catching his robe on the rail. He went down hard, but recovered admirably, quickly heaving his bulk up from the stage floor. He limped to Bosa, who had drawn himself up to full height. Brother John held out his arms in a gesture of peace, but the pagan chief only sneered with exaggerated disdain, shaking his head.

"*The chief priest of their idolatry started to curse God's people,*" Brother Elias read, his voice ringing. "*One of the bishop's companions took a stone which Bishop Wilfrid had blessed, and hurled it like David from a sling. It pierced the pagan's forehead through to the brain. Death took him as it took Goliath, unawares, and he fell back lifeless on the sand.*"

Bosa went down like an oak tree, rocking the stage so forcefully the canons wobbled on their feet, making the audience chuckle. He lay very still, playing dead, but Constance saw him open an eye and wink at Eilaf, who hooted with pleasure, earning a scowl from his grandmother. The horde of pagans now prepared to attack Wilfrid and his companions as they prayed for God's favorable intervention, kneeling with their hands raised to the heavens.

Suddenly, Bosa started to rise, staring hard at something in the audience. The canons hesitated, looking at each other with puzzled expressions. Then Brother John, improvising, jumped on Bosa's back, shouting, "You are dead, wicked pagan chief. The hand of God has smote you!"

Bosa paid no attention to the canon's cue, but continued to stand up, pointing. Brother John held fast like a tick. "Dead I say!" he shouted, beating on Goliath's immense shoulder. The audience laughed uproariously at the pig-a-back canon, thinking it was all part of the play.

Constance followed Bosa's outstretched arm, gasping when she saw to whom it pointed. In the audience, Master Gruffydd was clawing at his throat, head thrown back, eyes bulging. Those around were oblivious, riveted by the action on stage. Constance turned to Godwin, but he was already on his feet, shouting the merchant's name.

The audience stared in bewilderment at their bailiff as he raced toward them. The canons on stage halted when they heard his shouts. Constance ran to Brother Paul, calling for candles. Suddenly, cries broke out as those near Gruffydd finally understood his distress. His arms were now flailing, sending nearby cups and utensils crashing to the floor. Just as Godwin reached the merchant, he toppled backward from the bench. His body went rigid, then began to jerk with violent spasms. People backed away, including Maegden, who held one hand tightly over her mouth, the other clutching her sister's arm. Godwin knelt at Gruffydd's side, joined by Hafren, who had disentangled herself from her sister's grasp. Then Fara came, shoving her way through a knot of mesmerized onlookers. Gruffydd's eyes were rolled back in his head, his teeth tightly clenched, mouth oozing saliva. "Pry his mouth open!" Fara cried.

Constance and Brother Paul raced over with candles in their arms and hastily began lighting them. Brother Elias arrived as well, with several gaping canons on his heels. He quickly knelt at the merchant's side, saying, "Fetch the oil and holy water, Brother John." When the canon did not move, he shouted, "Now!" and Brother John snapped to attention. Brother Elias began chanting rapidly.

Godwin was grasping the merchant's jaw, trying desperately to open his mouth, but in vain. Blood streamed from wounds made by teeth biting flesh. Godwin's hands became slick, making it impossible to get a grip.

Brother Elias prayed faster, crossing himself swiftly every few moments. Beads of sweat gathered on his brow as he rushed on. Panting, Brother John arrived with a brass mazer of holy water and a small clay vial. Without looking up, Brother Elias grasped them, setting down the water to unstopper the vial. He anointed Gruffydd's eyes, ears, nostrils, lips, and hands. He was careful not to hinder Godwin and Fara's efforts. He never interrupted his stream of prayers.

Fara pulled her scarf from her head and pressed it to the flow of blood. Then, just as Brother Elias gasped out "amen," Gruffydd gave a great heave and went still. The hall was silent as Fara put a hand to his chest. After a few moments, she said, "He is gone." All made the sign of the cross.

Brother Elias sighed like a man who has pulled a child from a burning house. But Godwin continued to stare at the merchant, waiting for him to show some sign of life, despite the healer's pronouncement. He looked up at the ring of stunned faces. Maegden's was buried in the shoulder of her brother-in-law as she quietly sobbed. Brother Elias drew the eyelids closed, hiding the eerie whites of Gruffydd's eyeballs.

Hafren and Fara remained at the merchant's side, heads lowered. Looking from one to the other Godwin quietly observed, "Master Gruffydd was not prone to fits." The women's eyes met over the body, and they shook their heads.

Fara said, "Let us find his drinking vessel."

Constance and Brother Elias held candles aloft while Godwin searched the floor around Gruffydd's body. He retrieved a cup that still contained some bits of root and green leaves. Fara examined them closely and put her nose to the rim, smelling what remained of the contents before passing it to Hafren. The midwife's eyes widened when she, too, held the cup to her nose, prompting Godwin to ask, "What is it?"

"Water hemlock," Hafren answered.

Fara's eyes met Godwin's. She said, "Master Gruffydd was poisoned."

ELEVEN ✚

The guild members filed slowly from the Calefactory. Maegden went, too, clinging mutely to her sister, no longer weeping. Hafren held a protective arm around her as they made their way from the hall with Bethoc. Lady Gunnilda took her leave as well. Godwin sent her with Eilaf and Bosa and three knights, but she wanted his company, pleading, "Take me yourself, my son."

"You know I cannot, Mother, but I will return to Dilston as quickly as possible," he promised. She went without further protest, leaning heavily on her grandson and Bosa.

Fulk offered to escort Constance to Bordweal, but she curtly refused. Shrugging, he gave a big yawn and said, "I'm off to my quarters, then." Calling to Brother Mark, he ordered food and drink to be sent there, adding, "The master might have waited till we'd supped before turning up his toes."

When all but the canons had departed, Godwin, Constance, Fara, and Brother Elias went first to the priory kitchen. The cook, Brother Peter, was asked to join them, for Godwin wanted above all to find the deadly herb that had found its way into Gruffydd's drinking vessel. Brother Elias instructed the remaining canons to pray for the merchant's soul until they returned. When Godwin looked back, the monks were huddled together, staring uncertainly at the dead man.

Once in the kitchen, Fara surveyed the cluttered room. Her eyes roved quickly over the worktables still heaped with parings and dirty pots, coming to rest finally on a stout cutting block in the corner. On it lay the chopped remains of a leafy green herb and bits of root. Godwin followed as she went to examine the plant. "It is water hemlock," she confirmed, shaking her head in disbelief. "How did it come to be here?"

Godwin turned to the canon. "Brother?"

He was standing near a table crowded with platters of food meant for the feast. Next to him stood Brother John, who had trailed them to the kitchen, no doubt in hopes of garnering details that might be gossiped over later. He was absently nibbling on a meat pie, his expression pensive.

"Brother Peter? The herb?" Godwin repeated.

"Herb?" the canon repeated. He was a good-natured man with pleading brown eyes and a dusting of white whiskers on loose jowls.

"Yes, how did it come to be in your kitchen?"

"The master's herb? Why, he brought it himself. Said he wanted it steeped in a tea."

"A tea?" Fara said, frowning. "But it is poison."

Brother Peter's frightened eyes darted from Fara to Godwin. "He said it was a remedy. He ordered it served just before supper, while folk were having their ale."

"Who prepared it?" Godwin asked.

"I did, lord." His watery eyes suddenly grew wide. "I only did as Master Gruffydd asked. I did not know the herb was deadly!"

"Of course you didn't," Godwin assured him, staring thoughtfully at the remains of the herb.

"Lord Bailiff," Brother John suddenly cried, his mouth stuffed with pie crust and chopped meat. "I know where it came from! The leech gave Master Gruffydd the herb at the fair today. I was there! I saw the whole business!"

Godwin suddenly remembered Gruffydd grasping the stalks of a lacy plant.

Fara was shaking her head. "The leech? I cannot believe it."

Brother John, wiping buttery hands on his habit, eagerly gave them the details. "It is true! I was right behind the merchant in the leech's queue. The master complained of a sour stomach, and I *saw* the healer give him the herb. He said to use it as a tea to drink before supping. Poor Master Gruffydd drank his tea and now he is dead! The leech killed him!"

Godwin looked inquiringly at Fara, who said, "I did advise the master to consult the leech. He had a sore stomach and the mugwort I gave him did little good. But a man of healing would not dispense water hemlock."

When they returned to the Calefactory, Godwin sent Brother Thomas after Wulfstan. "Ask him to fetch the leech."

Constance remained with Brother Elias while Godwin and several of the canons bore Gruffydd from the Calefactory to the infirmary. His body, now slack and yielding, was heavy and difficult to manage in the dimly lit arcade encircling the Cloister Garth. Fara opened a door and the somber litter bearers awkwardly carried their burden into a large derelict room smelling of mildew.

The infirmary, part of a series of structures binding the cloister on its westerly side, was rarely used now, for its function as a place of ministration had been transferred to the hospital of St. Giles beyond the walls of the abbey. But Godwin could recall a time when a fire burned year-round in its hearth and a canon skilled in medicine stood continually by to care for the infirm and aged. As in the nearby lavatory, water could be drawn through a water-cock overhanging a stone trough, making it a fitting place to tend the dead.

They hoisted the body onto a slab table and removed all the clothing save Gruffydd's tunic. The canons took the soiled items to the trough and then returned to cleanse the merchant's face of blood.

Stripped of his rich garments and proud will, his sideways

glances and labored breathing, he seemed to Godwin shorn of his very identity, rendered a stranger. He might be anyone —a highborn bishop or a simple farmer. We are all equal in death, Godwin reflected, and foreign to those who knew us.

Fara bent to peer inside the merchant's mouth. She saw small leaves and pieces of root stuck between his teeth and under his tongue. She extracted enough to examine then held them out in the palm of her hand for the others to see. There was no question as to how the merchant died. "The herb brings on violent fits and kills its victims immediately," she said, pointing to the bits of yellow pulp, "especially if the root is consumed. It is the deadliest part of the plant."

Leaving the corpse in the care of the canons, they returned to the Calefactory where Godwin stoked the fire in the great hearth. Despite the evening's warmth, the four remaining in the hall huddled in their wraps, pulling them closer as if they could not get warm.

When the fire was bright, Brother Elias rose to snuff out several of the candles to conserve their wax. Godwin went out to gather more wood from the stack in the cloister, though the roaring fire needed no more fuel.

As a soldier and crusader, he had seen the deaths of many—had witnessed killings both slow and tortuous and quickly savage. Always he was disturbed by death, by how quickly it could seize a person. Yet with Gruffydd's passing he felt something more. It was pity, he realized, and, oddly, shame—a sense of dishonor on Gruffydd's behalf for the indignity of such a death. Godwin wondered at his reaction. The merchant, a pompous and churlish man, was an acquaintance by necessity only. But he had come to know a different man, not exactly likable, but . . . understandable. And knowing of his wife's faithlessness made Godwin all the more sorry.

Wulfstan finally arrived. He came with eyes gleaming and sword drawn, following on the leech too closely. The healer was composed, unmindful of the deputy's menacing bearing and the sword directed at his back. "I found him in the *tavern*," Wulfstan said, as if this in itself were an indictment.

Godwin gestured for the leech to take a seat. His slack mouth and reddened eyes testified to a wearying day and the late hour. The bailiff wasted no time. He placed the water hemlock, now wrapped in a rag, before the leech. Uncovering the herb, he said, "A man was poisoned tonight." The leech stared down at the herb, his wing-like brows drawing together over a hawkish nose. "Did you give this herb to Master Gruffydd at the fair today?" Godwin asked.

He raised his red-rimmed eyes. "I gave no one water hemlock."

"But you gave our Master Gruffydd something. What was it?"

The leech lifted his shoulders. "I ministered to many today."

Godwin described the merchant, seeing recollection kindle in the old man's eyes. "Yes, I remember," he said. "He had a stomach ailment and . . . another concern. I gave him the healing plant of the archangel—angelica. It is the best remedy for ulcers of the stomach."

Fara commented, "Water hemlock resembles angelica, and they grow in like places—marshes and moist meadows."

"Could you have confused them?" Godwin asked.

The leech gazed long at Fara and Godwin before offering a reply. "Little success would I have in my trade if I knew not water hemlock from angelica."

"Do you have the deadly herb in your possession?"

He shook his head. "Nay, it is too lethal."

"I must make certain," Godwin said. The healer acquiesced without protest, reaching for a key on a string around his neck. Turning to Wulfstan, Godwin said, "It is too dark now —we'll search the stall at dawn, before the fair opens." Turning back to the leech, he asked, "Where are you lodging?"

He was renting a room over the tavern. Godwin instructed his deputy to escort him back and leave the man in peace. Wulfstan's expression was severely disapproving.

When they had gone, Godwin sat down heavily. He realized he would have to stay over in the Moot Hall if he wanted to search the leech's stall at first light. Breaking the silence that had descended, he said, "Friends, what are your thoughts?"

No one spoke at first. The fire was burning hard and needed no prodding, yet Fara lifted a poker and stabbed at the logs, saying, "It is hard to suppose that a leech could mistake water hemlock for angelica."

Constance stared at the flying sparks set loose with each of Fara's jabs. "He is old. Perhaps he became confused."

"I suppose it is possible," Fara conceded. "Water hemlock resembles several plants that are prized and commonly sought, including water parsnip, wild caraway, and, of course, angelica. I've witnessed several cases of accidental poisoning and have heard of many more." Still, she looked doubtful, and Godwin guessed her mind: a life-long practitioner of healing was unlikely to confuse these herbs.

Though it was close to Matins by Godwin's reckoning, he had one more call to make now that Constance and Fara were safely returned to their homes. He was weary and craved sleep, yet he would not delay this errand. It brought him to the priory once more and had nothing to do with Master Gruffydd's death.

Once beyond the gatehouse, where the snores of Brother Michael loudly emanated, Godwin headed for the guest quarters situated near the courtyard at the cathedral's west entrance. He knew which room was Fulk's, for he always took the grandest, a commodious suite reserved for visiting dignitaries.

He rapped twice upon the door and waited, and when no one stirred, knocked again more loudly. Finally, Godwin heard movement followed by a hushed exchange of words. Then the door was thrown wide to reveal Fulk wearing only a knee-length tunic. His dark hair was tousled although he appeared wide-awake with no sign of sleep in his eyes. Godwin looked beyond for the servant he had addressed, but saw no one, only the remains of a meal and two goblets.

Fulk smiled, waving him into the room, saying, "Come."

But Godwin remained on the threshold. "I want a private word with you, Fulk." He looked across the room to the narrow arched way leading to a private chamber.

Fulk glanced over his shoulder, then back at Godwin, saying with an even wider grin, "Don't be troubled by her presence. She cares nothing for whatever you have to say."

"By God's eyeballs, Fulk!" Godwin exploded. Then he lowered his voice to a harsh whisper. "You would bring a harlot here?"

Fulk laughed until tears welled. "Ah me," he said, wiping his eyes. "You are rare, indeed, my friend. You would lower your voice to spare the feelings of a whore!"

Godwin only glared, and Fulk finally reined in his mirth, adding, "Prostitutes are no strangers to St. Andrews. Or did you not know?" He came outside, pulling the door firmly closed behind him. "But she is no harlot, I assure you. A gentlewoman is my companion this night. Her husband sits rotting in a Scottish prison, even as we speak, and she's desperate to win him back. I've the archbishop's ear, and she knows I can sway him to intervene."

Godwin gazed contemptuously at him. "And you would force her to your bed in exchange for influence?"

Fulk laughed heartily once more. "It was her proposal, you innocent, not mine! Though I admit, I put up little resistance. Still, I did protest, for I am all but betrothed to the fair Constance—"

Fulk neatly sidestepped Godwin's fist as it flew toward his face, but as he moved aside, the bailiff checked his swing and shot out the other hand to catch Fulk's throat in an iron grip. They were no match for one another. Godwin was lithe and strong, Fulk, a sleek feline whose defense lay in stealth and cunning.

Holding him to the door, Godwin said through clenched teeth, "You will end this game with Lady Constance. She will never be your wife." His hand dropped from the slender neck, though he stood menacingly close, awaiting Fulk's response.

For once, the man had no mocking reply to offer, no amused rejoinder. Indeed, an even rarer thing happened: Fulk's expression became sober, his voice sincere. "That I cannot do, my friend. I care deeply for the lady and will not withdraw my proposal." He flinched as Godwin's hands balled into fists, and hastened to add, "I know you hold her in the highest esteem, but you delay too long. If you will not make her your wife, I will, for I love her."

Now it was Godwin's turn to laugh, a ringing outburst that filled the silent night. Fulk's mouth tightened. He gazed at Godwin with bored disdain. "My declaration amuses you?"

Still chuckling, Godwin said, "You had me fooled, truly you did. I believed your proposal was sincere, but now I know it is false. You have no interest in wedding Lady Constance. I don't know what you are planning, but I'll wager it has nothing to do with a marriage portion."

"You are obviously exhausted, my friend. Of course I mean to *have* her." He grinned, raising a brow.

Godwin struggled to suppress his rage. "If you had expressed a desire for the wealth and lands she controls, then your marriage proposal would seem genuine. Ambitious men marry only for the assets and titles a lady can bring. You, with the archbishop's influence, could do far better—a duchess, or even an illegitimate child of royalty." Fulk's eyes flickered and Godwin knew his words hit close to the mark. "But you speak of caring and love, sentiments contrary to your nature. You are up to something—I care not what, only that you cease this charade. Will you do it?"

"Nay, I cannot," Fulk insisted. "Despite your opinion of

my character, I am quite capable of affection." His wounded look made Godwin's lips twitch. "But your words are more accurate than you realize. I am not her only suitor at the archbishop's court, for she *is* a prize worth wrangling over— Wait! Hear me out! Not only is the lady noble, but young and capable of bearing many more sons. Granted, she's a bit strong-willed and outspoken, but a husband can correct those flaws. More to the point, her son, a mere babe, stands to inherit Lord Eilan's barony. When Lady Constance weds, control of the lordship will pass to the husband until the son reaches manhood. *If* he does."

Godwin felt a hard, cold hand move down his spine. Quietly he said, "You speak of my godson, Fulk. Explain yourself and tread warily."

Fulk shrugged. "Only that life is uncertain. Many children do not survive to see their inheritance. It is common enough. And even if he does, it is many years away. In the meantime, a husband can wield the assets.

"So you see," he laughed, "I *am* the fortune-seeker you know me to be. And there are far worse than me courting the archbishop for the same prize. Yes, I could do better, but I am fond of Constance, and though she does not know it, she and her boy need protecting. Does she really find me so despicable?"

Godwin laughed, despite his mounting alarm, for the image of Fulk as a fretful vassal of love was too irresistible. But he soon sobered. "What kind of men are these? Constance is no horse to be traded. No one can press her into marriage, though I grant you, Lord Eilan will have much to say in the matter, for she holds from him."

Fulk slowly shook his head. "You do not know the ways of power, my friend. It is an ugly business, and the wishes of a woman are inconsequential. What kind of men are they? Let me just say that if she could chose, she would find *me* the least offensive!

"But she cannot. I paid dearly for this favor and my lord archbishop keeps his bargains. He has dispatched a letter to

Eilan in Dunbar. I know the contents, for I wrote it myself. Lord Eilan owes for old favors. The debt must now be repaid."

"And if Eilan refuses?" Godwin asked.

Fulk laughed. "Who would refuse the most powerful man in the north? Who would incur his wrath, risking lands and wealth for a mere woman?"

TWELVE ✝

A dawn chorus of birds awakened Godwin. After a hasty splash of cold water to his face, he left the Moot Hall, groggy and out of sorts. He had not slept well. Fulk's words haunted him the night through, and they troubled Godwin. He must speak with Constance. This business with Fulk and the archbishop was more serious than he had first thought. And yet, it was an awkward topic to broach.

When he had descended to the haugh, Godwin found it blanketed by a thick mist, seeing no farther than four or five booths in any direction. Away in the fog, the river sounded strangely close, its dwindling summer flow passing softly over cobbles and boulders.

Fara and Wulfstan were already at the leech's booth, huddled in their be-dewed capes. Godwin took the lock from the stall door, a rusty thing hardly worth the effort of employing. He and Fara entered the cramped space while Wulfstan remained outside. Godwin went to open the shutter to let in the pale light as Fara began her inspection. At first she found nothing out of place, but when her eyes turned upward to the bunches of herbs hanging from pegs in the low rafters, they opened wide.

Following her gaze, Godwin saw nothing unusual, only weedy plants smelling faintly pleasant, like hay or rushes. Fara reached up and took down two bundles, each containing several stalks still attached to their roots. Laying them side by side she pointed to one bundle, then the other saying, "This is water hemlock, this angelica."

The foliage of angelica and water hemlock were indeed similar, however, Godwin could see that their roots were quite different: those of angelica were thick, fleshy, and spindle-shaped while the roots of water hemlock were plump, yellowish tubers. Fara, staring in dismay, said, "He must have confused them after all."

"Aye, it must be so," Godwin agreed. "He is old—perhaps his sight is failing. We know little of this man."

"He has traveled widely, or so I have been told, even to the East. The infidels are great healers, you know."

Godwin stared at the herbs, noting that the water hemlock, though wilted, appeared fresher than the angelica. "When do you suppose these herbs were harvested?"

Fara studied the plants, considering. "The water hemlock was not gathered longer than a day ago, I would think, and yet . . . see how the plants are still attached to their roots? They would keep a bit longer than cut stalks. . . . I suppose they could have been pulled from the ground two or three days ago. The angelica was pulled much earlier. See how the leaves are curling and beginning to brown?"

"Yes," Godwin said, bending closer to examine the bulbs of the water hemlock. Growing from them were thick clusters of hair-like roots still clinging to bits of dark soil. "I wonder," he said, pointing. "This earth is still moist, and it has been warm and dry these past weeks. If the water hemlock was collected two or three days ago, the soil clinging to the roots should be dust by now."

"Yes," Fara agreed. "It must have been only yesterday then. But why is it important to know when the plants were gathered?"

"I'm not sure," Godwin said, straightening. Glancing around the stall, he saw a burlap sack. "Come, let's gather up the water hemlock before it can do more harm."

As Godwin replaced the lock on the stall door, he told Wulfstan to take Fara home, and then bring the leech to the Moot Hall. When his deputy's eyes gleamed with hostile satisfaction, he warned, "Take care, Wulfstan. No bullying. Nothing is known for sure, and he's an old man. Deal gently with him."

Godwin returned to the Moot Hall with the sack slung over his shoulder, passing early risers heading for the fair and good bargains. When he had made the ascent to the Market Square, he found it growing busy and flooded with sunshine. He stood a moment to savor its warmth. As he turned to enter the Moot Hall, he saw an officer of the guild, Edward the baker, Master Gruffydd's deputy. "My lord," Edward said, "have you any news? Did the leech kill Master Gruffydd? Everyone is saying so!"

"Come inside, Edward," Godwin said, for several people were staring curiously, ears pricking. The baker followed Godwin into the hall where he waited, twisting his hands together. Loose-limbed and lean, Edward had long, fluttering fingers that knotted like tangled rope when he became nervous.

Godwin sat near the cold hearth and gestured for Edward to take a seat opposite. The Moot Hall is a cavernous room, capable of accommodating the many who appeared at his monthly court as jurors and litigants. It was stoutly built and easy to defend, but wickedly cold, no matter the season. Godwin yearned for a fire, or the sunshine outside, but pulled his cape closer instead and turned to Edward, saying, "I know nothing for certain yet, saving that Master Gruffydd was poisoned."

The baker's brows were arched high over bulging eyes. "The leech! Brother John is saying he gave Master Gruffydd an evil remedy."

Godwin said nothing as Edward reached up to smooth the four or five strands of hair that graced an otherwise gleaming head, saying, "He gave me a tonic for my hair. Do you suppose it is safe?"

The door of the Moot Hall flew open, sending the man from his bench. Wulfstan, not gently, nudged the leech into the hall. Godwin glared at his deputy then used the opportunity to conclude his conversation with the baker, who was staring fearfully at the healer. "I'll keep you informed, Edward. I assume you are heading up the guild now?"

The baker blanched. "I suppose I am," he quavered, drawing a revolted look from Wulfstan. "Then it is up to me to arrange Master Gruffydd's funeral!"

"Yes, and you will no doubt want to consult his wife as well as the acting prior."

The baker scuttled from the hall, his narrow shoulders stooped under the mantle of sudden responsibility. Godwin turned to Wulfstan. "I need you to fetch Asheferth, and I've no idea where he is." His deputy nodded once, then spun on his heel and marched out, slamming the door.

"Feral, that one," the leech commented.

Godwin gestured to the bench vacated by the baker. Then he busied himself with lighting a fire. The leech, wearing the same threadbare gown he'd worn the day before, shuddered every few moments. Over his shoulder, Godwin said, "He's been at my side through many tight spots, and I was always thankful for it afterwards! He's fierce in battle."

"Have you been in many battles as Bailiff of Hexham?" the leech asked, his tone amused.

"A local siege or two. But Wulfstan has been with me long before I was bailiff."

"Ah, yes, I've heard from the locals that you were once a crusader." He studied Godwin. "Not King Richard's crusade, you would have been too young. Damietta?"

Godwin sat down. "Yes. Now, I have some questions for *you*, master leech. Water hemlock was found in your stall." He pointed at the sack on the floor. "It was hanging among angelica, the herb you claim to have given Master Gruffydd. Last night you said you didn't keep the herb on hand. How do you account for its presence in your stall?"

The leech's gray eyes were rested this morning—clear and

alert—amused even. He did not appear surprised. "A riddle to be sure."

"This is no light matter," Godwin warned. "A man is dead, and it is quite likely *you* gave him the poisonous herb."

"Nay, I did not give your merchant water hemlock, either mistakenly or maliciously."

"But it was found it in your booth. Is it not *possible* you made an error, collected and dispensed a deadly herb, thinking it was angelica?"

"They are alike to the untrained eye, but not to mine," the leech insisted.

"Then how did the water hemlock come to be in your stall if you did not put it there?"

The leech shrugged. "Is that not for you to discover?"

Godwin's eyes narrowed. "Are you suggesting someone else did?" The leech was silent. "Why?" Godwin asked

"Can you not guess, Lord Bailiff?"

"I do not guess, nor speak in riddles. When did you last gather herbs for your stores?"

"Near York. I have been gathering for some time, in preparation for the fair."

The leech was lucid and composed, almost too composed given the gravity of the situation. "Tell me," Godwin said, "where is your birthplace?"

"Not far from here—Flixton."

Godwin's eyebrows went up. Yorkshire. He hadn't expected the leech to be a Northerner. "Kin?"

"I'm the son of a monk whose duty it was to tend the sick at the hospital of Flixton. My mother died bringing me into this world, and my father raised me. He was a learned man and a good master." He shuddered again, and Godwin stood up to prod the fire. "Nay, it is not the cold that makes my body quake," he said. "Your fire does me good, but it cannot cure my sickness."

"What ails you?"

He shrugged bony shoulders. "It is a mystery, even to one as learned as I. The illness comes and goes. Today it is bad.

Tomorrow might be better."

"Traveling must be difficult."

"Yes, but I do not roam far these days."

"You did once, or so I have heard. When did you first leave Flixton?" Godwin asked, getting back to piecing the man's life together.

"I was not destined to become a man of the cloister like my father, but I took minor orders to continue my studies. A bishop became my patron—I cured him of an illness and he recognized my skill. He sent me to Paris, where I studied the works of the Greeks. From there I traveled to Spain and Italy and still farther to the East."

They sat in silence. Finally the leech said, "There is more to tell concerning my dealings with the merchant." He told Godwin of Gruffydd's suspicion that his wife was having an affair, how he had given him the two flowers—the lily and the rose—along with the angelica for his ulcer, to test her fidelity. Godwin's mind went back to the previous day, to the strange scene at Gruffydd's booth. The merchant had learned of his wife's unfaithfulness, and then he had died.

THIRTEEN ⚔

*T*he women helped Yves to the maid's bed, situated behind a curtain hung across the lady's chamber. They tended his wound, bringing water in a golden vessel to wash his thigh, binding it with a white silk cloth. When the evening meal was brought, they secretly shared it with the knight. Yves ate and drank well.

Yet as the days passed and his injury healed, Yves was struck by another—a growing love for Nicolette. He sighed with a new anguish, and when the maid came to care for him, he begged her to go, wanting to be alone with his distress. Yves laid awake night after night, turning over in his mind Nicolette's words and appearance, her bright eyes and fair mouth. "Alas," he thought, "what shall I do? Should I confess my love to her? What if she refuses me? I'll die of grief!"

The knight did not know that Nicolette was afflicted by the same illness, or he might have suffered less. The maid, however, could see they were in love, and when her mistress went to church one morning, she told Yves, "My lord, you are in love. Take care not to hide it too well, for the love you offer might be well received." Yves was greatly emboldened by the revelation, and when the lady came that evening to see how he fared, he *confessed his love.*

The knight stayed with Nicolette for many months, and their lives were filled with pleasure, due in large part to the maid who watched over the lovers and guarded their secret. But Fortune never fails to turn her wheel, raising one soul up while casting down another, and so it happened with Yves and Nicolette.

One summer morning, as the lady was laying beside her young lover, she said to him, "My love, my heart tells me that I am going to lose you. We will be discovered and you will be forced to leave. And when you do, you will find another love, while I stay on here in misery."

"Lady, do not say such things! I could never find joy with another!"

"Do you promise?" When he nodded, she took his shirt and put a knot in the tail, making it in such a way that no other woman could untie it except with scissors or knife. Handing it back to Yves, she said, "You have my leave to love the woman, whoever she may be, who is able to unbind this knot."

He took the shirt, but made her give a similar pledge by means of a belt. She must wear it next to her bare flesh, tightened about her flanks. He urged her to love the one who could open the buckle without breaking it or severing it from the belt.

That day they were discovered—spied upon and found out by an evil chamberlain. . . .

FOURTEEN ✟

W hen Burchard appeared in the doorway of the Moot Hall, Godwin was sorting through writs from the archbishop and was happy for the interruption. Like Wulfstan, he was a loyal knight, long in Godwin's service. However, the less demanding duties associated with service in Hexhamshire were beginning to tell. He was growing round and rarely suited up in armor. Still, he carried a well-tended sword, sheathed in a belt cinched beneath an ample belly.

He had come to give a report on his watch at the fair the previous night. "Any disturbances?" Godwin asked.

"No lord. The night was quiet. It was an easy watch under a full moon."

Eilaf and Bosa interrupted them when they noisily entered the Moot Hall carrying a large basket covered by a cloth. Godwin looked closely at his nephew, but saw no signs of last night's horror on his youthful face.

Godwin smelled fresh bread and roasted chicken and suddenly took notice of his empty stomach. "The saints bless my mother," he said, relieving Bosa of the burden. "She's forgiven my absence it would seem. Burchard, join us."

"Nay, I'm off to bed," he yawned.

When he was gone, Godwin asked, "How is Grandmother today?"

Eilaf pulled a face. "Thorny! She sent us here because we

would not scrub furniture."

"Scrub furniture? Why would she ask you to do that?" Godwin sat down with the basket and started in on the chicken.

"*Everything's* been taken from the house—tables, benches, chests, beds—everything, Uncle! She wants the whole lot scrubbed and oiled, and everyone has been ordered to help."

"Why take the furniture outside?" Godwin asked, pausing with a drumstick halfway to his mouth.

Eilaf shrugged. "The servants are scrubbing the floors, and I think she means to have the walls whitewashed."

"Perhaps I'll stay in the Moot Hall another night," Godwin said, reaching for more chicken. "Poor Burchard. He'll get no rest today." He wiped his face and hands on the cloth, and then rose to pour some wine. Tearing off a hunk of bread, he asked, "What of your studies, Nephew? Will you be reading and writing here today, or did you think you might spend another day at the fair?"

Eilaf glanced longingly at the door. "I cannot study at Dilston," he explained. "It is too confused. Besides, Grandmother sent me away." He grinned, having reckoned all the points in his favor.

Godwin rooted in the basket for something else and found a plum. "It's time we paid Brother Elias a visit. Bosa, you'll come, too. Later, we shall all go to Bordweal."

As they left the Moot Hall, Eilaf sprinted ahead on a sudden burst of youthful energy. Bosa loped to catch up while Godwin picked up his pace, thinking about a visit to Bordweal with a jolt of pleasure. How sturdy we are, he reflected, gazing at the animated crowd in the Market Square, capable of joy in the very wake of death.

They found Brother Elias sitting at a large desk in a private chamber designated for the prior's use, pouring over yellowed charters written in fading ink. The room was spacious and grandly furnished, for many of his predecessors had been eager to display their status. Brother Elias, however, looked incongruous amidst the lavish surroundings.

He grew flustered when he saw Godwin, white cheeks blurring to pink. Once they were all seated, he hastened to explain, "I'm cataloging the priory's holdings, and the charters are stored here." He waved a hand toward a gilded chest filled with parchment rolls.

Godwin said, "You've every right to occupy this space, brother, for you are acting prior." The canon nodded, sinking back into a vast chair sporting carvings of angels blowing trumpets.

Brother Elias asked, "How is the young widow?"

"I've not seen her yet. She's with her sister's family."

"Poor soul." He looked down at his hands. "We'll need to bury her husband very soon—with summer and all."

"The baker is handling it. He'll be coming to see you." Godwin gestured to the parchments. "This inventory, did the archbishop request it?"

"Nay, it is a feeble attempt to understand my responsibilities as prior. I must know the specifics of our holdings if the properties are to be managed properly."

"Is there no such list already?" Godwin knew the lands owned by St. Andrews were extensive, if poorly managed. To catalogue them would be a daunting task indeed.

"Alas, Brother John tells me it is lost or destroyed. But no matter," he said, brightening, "for it has been a valuable lesson. I have been through the charters once already. Now I am arranging them by region, for an idea has occurred to me." He spoke keenly now, unaware that Eilaf and Bosa were beginning to fidget. "The lands held by this priory are far flung, as you know, lord, and leasing so many estates should be enormously profitable, yet this establishment is poor." Godwin nodded, wishing Brother Elias would come to the point. "I think it is because our lands are so far-flung, sprinkled throughout the north. It is impossible to efficiently oversee them." He stopped, awaiting a response.

Godwin groped for one, not wanting to disappoint. "Well, it's a common enough predicament among great landholders. Is that not why they employ stewards?"

"Yes, yes, I have traveled far to meet with several stewards hired into service by former priors of this institution, and none even recalled the name St. Andrews! They will comply for a time, now they have been reminded, but only for a time. Eventually, the rents will stop coming and another long journey will have to be undertaken. No, the answer, I have discovered, lies in consolidation."

Godwin stared blankly. Bosa stretched his tree-like limbs and yawned. Eilaf rose from his chair to begin an exploration of the room.

Brother Elias hurried on. "I intend to sell or exchange property that is farther than a day's ride from here in order to purchase or acquire lands closer to St. Andrews." He rose to pace the room, thinking aloud, looking quite at home in the chamber. "Regular presence and oversight by myself and the cellarer will ensure the rents are paid. The added expense of hiring stewards will be eliminated in many cases. And I have other ideas! In my travels these last weeks, I've seen much fertile land nearby, capable of producing a wealth of food, once it has been cleared or drained. No doubt, this priory could buy these sorts of parcels cheaply. They'll make splendid investments!"

"Cleared or drained?" Godwin said faintly. "These are great tasks, brother. Who will do the labor?"

"Why, the canons of St. Andrews!"

Godwin could think of no encouraging reply, therefore, he said nothing. Try as he might, he could not summon an image of the canons toiling to bring raw land under cultivation. Finally, he said, "A worthy goal, brother. I suspect the archbishop will be pleased to hear of your plans."

Brother Elias's face sobered at the mention of his lord, and his attention suddenly focused on the others in the room. "What am I thinking! You are not here to speak of tenants and farming! Forgive me, lord."

"Do not apologize. I'm interested in your progress. After all, I recommended you to the archbishop. It pleases me to know you will worthily fill the post, should he confirm you." Brother Elias cast his eyes down, cheeks flushing pink again. "But there is a favor I wish to ask," Godwin continued, "though I hesitate now that I see how hard at work you are."

"Nay, ask away! Please! I would be honored to serve!"

"Well," Godwin said, "it concerns Eilaf." At the mention of his name, his nephew put down the quill he had been toying with to stand at his uncle's side. "He has exceeded the skills of his tutor, and yet I think the boy is capable of more. Would it be an imposition to take him on as your pupil?"

- 107 -

Brother Elias shifted his gaze to study Eilaf, who smiled tentatively. "I would be very pleased to instruct your nephew, lord," the canon said, giving Eilaf a reassuring smile in return. "Perhaps he can assist me with these charters and my scheme, though it may require him to accompany me now and then when I travel about the shire."

Eilaf beamed, then quickly looked at Bosa. Godwin said, "My deputy has duties of his own, nephew. The two of you can be parted for a few hours a day." Turning back to Brother Elias, he said, "I am most grateful brother—"

He was interrupted by Fulk, who burst into the room. "Good, you're both here," he said by way of salutation. "I'm leaving. There's trouble brewing among our worthy regents. Word is Bishop Peter's been ousted!" He rubbed his hands together. "The archbishop wants his best man at Westminster, with an ear cocked."

Godwin said dryly, "Sounds like the perfect job for you, Fulk—eavesdropping and gossip-mongering." But Godwin was relieved, and he motioned for Bosa and Eilaf to wait outside. "Will you end your charade with Lady Constance?" he asked when they had gone. "If you like, I can inform her of your departure."

"*Au contraire!*" Fulk sang. "Though she continues to deny it, the lady is mine. I shall return for her the moment my duties allow."

Godwin glanced at Brother Elias, who was fervently studying a charter. "Go now then, Fulk, before you suffer a painful accident."

He laughed. "Jealousy's a wicked sin, my friend. You'd best seek absolution." He gestured at Brother Elias.

Godwin charged, saying, "By God's eyeballs, I'll throttle you—" But he reigned in his rage when he saw Brother Elias's face.

"Steady, man!" Fulk laughed. "I'm going soon enough, but there's another matter." He was all business again, saying, "My justices will manage the faircourt, but they need another clerk. Brother Elias, can you produce one? Good." Turning back to the bailiff, he said, "They are wondering about the merchant's complaint? Will his kin prosecute, do you know, or should it be dismissed?"

Godwin's fury subsided. John Longspee and the merchant's suit had been driven clean from his mind. "I'll have to speak to Maegden."

"A tasty looking morsel, that one," Fulk commented. He laughed at Brother Elias' gasp. "How goes the inquiry?" When Godwin made no reply, Fulk added, "I'll wager the merchant was murdered by her lover."

A strangled noise came from Brother Elias, who excused himself from the room. Godwin eyed Fulk, saying, "What makes you think she has a lover?"

Fulk gazed pityingly at Godwin. "An obvious deduction, my friend." Then he left without a backward glance.

Godwin stepped out to join the others. Brother Elias breathed a sigh of relief, saying, "That man frightens me!"

"It would please him to know it." Godwin said, staring after Fulk.

"Is it true lord?" Brother Elias whispered. "Was the merchant murdered?"

Godwin went once more to the priory kitchen, sending Bosa and Eilaf to wait in the church while he spoke to the cook. He found both Brother John and Brother Peter beside the table heaped with last night's victuals, as if they had never departed.

"The guild members came and took away their food," Brother Peter hurried to explain when he saw the bailiff, "but I used the priory's stores to prepare these dishes, and they won't keep. *Something* must be done." He held up a half-eaten pudding.

"Brother Peter, I wanted to ask you about the tea again. When you handled the herb, could you say whether it was angelica or water hemlock?"

He shook his head. "I wouldn't know the difference, lord."

Godwin turned to Brother John. "You saw the leech give Master Gruffydd the herb at the fair. Did it look the same as what was found on the chopping block last night?"

The canon put down a sausage to consider, his face puckering with the effort. "I really do not know, lord. My mind wasn't on any herb."

"Who was near you in the line?" Godwin asked.

"Let me think. . . . Brother Thomas came after me. I think Brother Paul was next or was it Edward? No, it was Brother Paul, then Edward. . . ." He frowned, adding, "Aside from them, I couldn't say, lord. I was looking ahead, not behind."

Godwin turned back to Brother Peter. "Who else was in your kitchen last evening?"

"Who else? Why, who was *not* in my kitchen, lord! Every guild member traipsed through here, bringing food and beer, giving orders and the like. Servants, too. Those hired by the guild along with our own."

"Did you see anyone handling Master Gruffydd's herb?" The canon shook his head, white jowls wagging.

"Who served it once the tea was prepared?"

"I delivered it myself, lord. The servers were busy passing ale, and I didn't want the merchant stomping into my kitchen, bellowing for his tea! He was an impatient man, you know, God keep his soul."

Godwin was entering the west doors of the cathedral when he saw Wulfstan marching toward him. Waiting in the vestibule for his deputy, he heard peals of laughter from deep within the church.

Without preamble, his deputy reported, "I cannot find that wretched Asheferth anywhere, lord! I've asked the men and no one has seen him. He is hunting on his own, I reckon." Wulfstan's face curdled with disgust, for hunting was not normally a solitary pursuit. "Should I send some of the men to seek him?"

A shriek, followed by thudding feet echoed through the church, and Wulstan peered over his bailiff's shoulder into the nave. Whatever he saw made him shake his head.

"Nay," Godwin said, "he could be anywhere." But he was thinking Asheferth would not stray far from his lover.

He told Wulfstan to keep watch at the fair, and that if he was needed, to send for him at Bordweal, adding, "The leech's booth is to remained closed."

Godwin strode into the nave, stopping a moment to let his eyes adjust to the dim light. More peals of laughter filled the quiet interior, and Godwin caught a fleeting glimpse of his nephew bolting into the north transept. Bosa was standing near a pillar with his eyes closed, counting loudly. "Eilaf! Bosa!" he called sharply, stalking up the aisle. "Stop this game at once, do you hear!"

Bosa's eyes flew open while Eilaf crept from a chapel in the transept. "You ought to be ashamed!" Godwin scolded. "This is no way to behave in a church. If Brother Elias had found you instead of me, he'd likely reconsider his offer, Nephew."

"I'm sorry, Uncle," Eilaf said, his head hanging low with Bosa's.

"Out," Godwin growled. When they were in the sun's glare, he said, "Get the horses ready. Wait for me at the stable." He followed behind as they walked slowly to the gatehouse, slinking and shuffling. Godwin scowled whenever Eilaf dared a backward glance.

Outside the gates, the boys went left, while Godwin turned right toward the Market Square and Gruffydd's home. When he looked back, he saw they were running headlong down Gilesgate. Eilaf was in the lead, howling with laughter as he nimbly dodged the folk in the street. Bosa's path was more direct, and people hastily stepped aside as the deputy galloped by.

Godwin found two servants—a young boy and a girl—in the merchant's home, but no Maegden. She was with her sister at Bordweal, the girl nervously informed him as he stepped into a small anteroom. She kept a tense distance from him, eyes lowered. He followed them up a steep flight of stairs to the hall. "Show me the kitchen," he said. They started at his request, glancing nervously at one another. He knew them of course. The girl, about fourteen, was Emma, the other Malcolm, a lanky boy Eilaf's age. If he remembered right, they had entered service for Gruffydd when he bought the house on the square two years ago. They were familiar faces in Hexham, but now he thought about it, not as regular as one might expect. Gruffydd must have been a demanding master to keep them inside so much.

When he came into the kitchen, just beyond the hall, he understood their agitation. They had been seated on a bench at the table eating and drinking from their mistress's stores. Dirty crockery and tinware was strewn about, and the floor had not been swept. Ignoring all this, he asked, "Are there any fresh herbs here?"

His question puzzled them, but after a moment, Emma told him there had been no fresh herbs in the kitchen since market day over a week ago.

"Did your master bring home any herb or plant yesterday?"

In a low voice he could barely hear, Emma said, "We didn't

see our master yesterday, lord bailiff. We had the morning off to visit the fair. When we came back in the afternoon, he was not at home, nor did he return."

Gruffydd must have gone directly from the fair to St. Andrews. It was reasonable, Godwin reflected, given their late meeting with the justices at the faircourt. The merchant probably did not have time to return home before the festivities at the priory.

The children were waiting obediently for any other questions. Godwin suddenly took note of their gaunt faces and bony figures. How they contrasted with his own servants. "Your master, did he treat you fairly?"

Both nodded and he knew they were lying.

FiFTEEN

Constance was wandering the burned-out remains of Bordweal's chapel when Godwin arrived. She was with Hereberht, who radiated his disapproval with severe looks whenever his robe brushed against the mossy stones. Snatching it up, he would glare at the offending rubble, and then at his mistress as he dutifully trailed her.

She found the setting lovely, enchanting even, and a little sad, with its ruined chapel grown over in places by wild vines. A greensward, neatly shorn by sheep, served as paving for the half walls and tumbled arches. There was a tiny cemetery adjacent with a few tilted headstones, worn smooth by age and covered by brightly colored lichens.

It was perhaps lovelier now than it had been when whole, she reflected, studying the cut blocks at her feet. The stone had been simply, even crudely, sculpted, with no embellishment that she could detect. Her new chapel would be far more handsome. But she must first bring her steward around to the idea. Constance was mentally devising arguments when she saw Godwin walking swiftly toward them from the manor house.

When they greeted, she felt an uncomfortable fluttering in her limbs, making her glance away as their eyes met. Looking around, he asked, "What brings you out to these ruins?"

Delighted by the prospect of gaining a supporter, she said, "I'd like to rebuild the chapel, Godwin. Bordweal needs a church close by, as there once was. And it could serve those north of here who travel far to reach St. Andrews." Glancing at Hereberht, she bluntly added, "My steward thinks it would be a waste of my son's silver."

Godwin's eyebrows went up, and Hereberht hastened to defend his position. "The tenants are accustomed to attending Mass in town. It would be more practical to allot the resources to another worthy cause."

A diversion. Constance knew that Hereberht believed in no worthy causes save the preservation of wealth. "There was a chapel here once. Why not again?" When the steward made no reply, she turned to Godwin. "How did it burn down, do you know?"

"It happened long ago," Godwin said, "during William's reign. You've heard stories of Scotland's Lion? No? Well, we must remedy that. He's my kin, you know." Surveying the ruins again he said, "Scotland's kings were once glorious—I'll tell you and Aldwin their stories by an evening hearth if ever you like." Constance smiled.

"The story of this church is part of a larger tale, one that concerns Scotland's claims in the north. When William the Lion came to the throne, two generations or so before my birth, he met with King Henry in an effort to convince England's ruler to give back Northumbria to Scotland. Henry laughed, telling William the only way he would win the north was with an army. So William invaded. He timed his attack with the rebellion of Henry's sons.

"The raids were cruel. William's warriors burned and killed mercilessly—nobles, peasants and their crofts, stock—nothing was spared. Those who held from Scottish lords and loyal to her king were not molested. My mother's kin fought for William, but Bordweal belongs to the Gosforth clan, and they hold from England, as my father's kin. Bordweal, like Dilston Hall, was besieged. Its manors were spared because they were useful strongholds, but everything else was destroyed."

"But why burn churches?" Constance asked. "They should not be made to suffer when men war."

He shrugged. "But they always do."

Following a new thought, she asked, "Godwin, is it not difficult holding lands from two lords when one is the king of England, the other a Scot? How do you serve both loyalties?"

"It's not so hard these days, for our kings are at peace. Besides, King Alexander is all but a vassal of England." His voice sounded regretful. "But borders are fickle, especially on the Marches, and one must take care to render the services due each lord, no matter their quarter. If conflict arises, a choice must be made, but always the choice is clear."

"If *you* had to choose, which would it be—Scotland or England?"

He did not stop to consider, but his voice was grim when he said, "I hold Dilston, my patrimony, from England's king, and it is for him I must fight if ever the two war."

"But that would mean betraying your kin—your mother and Earl Patric."

He shook his head. "Marriage has mingled all the great houses of the north with Scotland's. You do not know because you're Wessex born. The royal houses, too, are joined. Alexander has married Joan, King John's sister."

He had not answered her question, but she didn't press it, asking instead, "Whatever became of William the Lion?"

Godwin grinned at her, his playful mood restored. "Have me to supper one evening, and I'll tell you the tale in full!"

"A fair exchange," she laughed.

They stood a moment longer, gazing at the chapel relics. "Now I know something of its history, more than ever I want to restore it. We should rebuild when men destroy, or our land would be a wretched place."

Godwin nodded. "It would be a goodly turn. I think Aidan would have done the same, had he been given the time." They looked at Hereberht who stiffly inclined his head.

* * *

"No news from Dunbar?" Constance asked as they walked the lane toward the manor.

"Nay, my messenger has not yet returned."

"I would like to go to Dunbar," Constance said. "It would cheer Galiena to see her grandson." She hesitated. "And . . . when my father-in-law is well enough . . . I'd like to discuss Fulk's proposal." Godwin did not reply, and Constance sensed his alert stillness as they continued to walk slowly. "I am the guardian of my son's inheritance, and my Lord Eilan would never agree to Fulk's wishes, whether the archbishop supports him or no. I wish to inform Lord Eilan of Fulk's scheming. He will know how to put an end to them."

"Yes," Godwin said. "I've been thinking the same. Eilan's sway is great in the north—a worthy equal of the archbishop. And yet . . . well, I hope he's soon well enough to act. When a great man is ailing much mischief can be done."

"But he is my lord. I cannot marry without his approval, for any man I marry will be the guardian of my son's inheritance."

"That's so," Godwin said. "Yet stories abound of women forced into marriage. Do not count on what's right and wrong, for law and custom are easily bent to the will of the powerful." He stopped their strolling to face her. "There is something else you must know." Godwin told her about the letter sent to Eilan by the archbishop. "I don't know how it will go, Constance. Eilan will do everything in his power to protect you, but it may not be enough."

Constance closed her eyes, willing herself not to cry. Godwin took both her hands, and when she opened her eyes his expression was hesitant, almost wary. "I've been giving this problem much thought," he said. "And I know a way to outwit Fulk."

"You do?" Constance cried. "Tell me!"

Carefully, he said, "In the laws of marriage, consent to wed is binding. I will swear that you and I pledged ourselves to one another prior to Fulk's proposal."

Constance felt a quick succession of emotions—joy, relief, puzzlement, suspicion, anger, and somewhere in the turmoil, a deep affection for the man who stood awkwardly before her. But as her mind made connections, the anger grew to crowd out all. She pulled her hands from his, asking coldly, "Did Cynwyse put you up to this?"

"Cynwyse?"

"Yes. She proposed the same scheme yesterday."

"I did not know! I've talked to no one, nor would I without first speaking with you."

"It does not matter. I will not take part in so callow a plot—marry one for the sole purpose of thwarting another. Nor am I on offer to the highest bidder! Marriage is a sacred union, Godwin, a sacrament."

"You misunderstand me! My sole purpose is not—wait, it's come out all wrong!" She turned away and Godwin hastened to follow, while Hereberht kept a cautious distance. "Constance, please wait!"

His dejected call made her stop and turn, and the anger dissolved as she watched him grope for words, fearful to say more, desperate to explain. Quietly she said, "I am grateful for your efforts, Godwin. I know I sought your help, but I will not right this wrong by using Fulk's methods. You see why?"

"Yes . . . No! What difference does it make, so long as you . . . do not marry Fulk?"

She smiled. "Your instincts tell you to help, but in this case, it is not your place."

"Constance, you must take help wherever it is offered. A woman's wishes are of no concern to men who hold power!"

"What *does* concern them?"

He thought a moment. "Silver."

"Silver," she slowly repeated as they passed the midwife's house, turning into Bordweal's orchard. The tension between them began to subside.

After a few moments, Godwin said, "There is a bit of good

news to report. Fulk was called from Hexham this morning. But he'll be back soon enough."

He was staring thoughtfully at Hafren's farmstead. It was quiet; none of the girls were at play in the croft. As they walked toward the garden at the orchard's edge, Constance said, "I can't believe the merchant is dead. Poor Maegden. How is she?"

"I cannot say. Her servants tell me she is with Hafren. I must seek her out, though it is a task I dread."

They sat on a shaded bench near Bordweal's large garden crowded with herbs, flowers, and vegetables. It was looking rather parched now, the plump lushness of June long by, yet its well-tended rows and small islands of color provided by yellow roses, purple asters, and fragrant lavender made it a pleasing sight to settle near.

Constance said, "It's hard to know how to comfort folk who are grieving." She remembered her own fresh days of misery, the stream of unwelcome well wishers and condolence givers. "Perhaps she needs a few days alone with her kin."

Godwin sighed. "That I cannot give." He told her what he had discovered concerning Gruffydd's death and the meaning behind the flowers they had seen the merchant give to Maegden at the fair. "Master Gruffydd had cause to be suspicious. She has a lover—my knight Asheferth." Constance nodded. "You're not surprised?" he asked.

"Nay, Gruffydd was much older and . . . not a comely man. Maegden is flighty and youthful. She was destined to grow unhappy in such a marriage."

Looking doubtful, Godwin said, "She must be twenty years of age, no child."

"Yes, old enough to have born her own. But Maegden is younger in mind than body. She has spent much time at Bordweal, and I've come to know her. Often I've thought she behaves more like a maid than a merchant's wife. And always she wants to hear stories of knights and love."

"Stories?"

"Yes, I read to my serving girls and the tenants' wives, as their chores allow. Tales of King Arthur and his knights are among their favorites."

"What story are you reading now?"

"'Yves and Nicolette.'"

Godwin wrinkled his nose and for a moment resembled Eilaf, making her laugh. He laughed with her and the last of the tension between them disappeared. "Such a silly tale! Why do women favor these stories?"

"Why do men compose them?" she countered. "Many gentlefolk, men and women both, take pleasure in romances. Why do *you* find them disagreeable?"

"Because they are misleading. Knights and ladies do not, *could not*, behave that way."

"Is that not the point—to enter briefly a fanciful world?" She stopped, struck by an idea. "Godwin! What if these stories encouraged Maegden to take up with your knight? They are about love, adulterous love—"

"Nay, don't think that! Knowing Asheferth, he was the hunter, she the hunted. Besides, Maegden knows right from wrong."

Constance stared at the garden, watching as Sidroc emerged from a row of beans. The beekeeper was growing smaller with the years, no bigger now than many of the taller crops. He waved when he saw them, then went back to his harvest. Constance said, "Surely you are not thinking they had something to do with the merchant's death? It was an accident, was it not, a mistake on the leech's part?"

"We found water hemlock in his booth, but the leech swears he never collected any. If what he claims is true, it means Gruffydd's angelica was deliberately switched for a deadly herb—"

"Murder?" Constance said, turning on the bench to face him.

"Perhaps." He told her about the leech's flimsy padlock, the moist soil clinging to the water hemlock. "What if someone wanted Gruffydd dead? They see him with the angelica and hit upon the idea of swapping it for water hemlock. The poisonous plant is gathered—Fara tells me it grows freely in the marshes nearby—and a switch made before the feast. Later in the night, the killer evades my watchmen at the fair site and breaks into the leech's stall to put the poisonous herb within to further implicate him. Gruffydd's death would be attributed to a deadly error on the part of the healer.

"And if it was murder," Godwin concluded, "Maegden and Asheferth are the likely culprits are they not? It is a common enough motive."

Constance was shaking her head. "No, Maegden is not capable, I'm sure of it."

"I agree, she is an unlikely murderer, yet love can incite terrible things."

"Perhaps it was your knight, acting alone."

Godwin rubbed his chin, feeling the stubble of several days' growth. "Maybe it was neither. Master Gruffydd may have had enemies I am not yet aware of. If he carried the angelica all over the fair, half of the shire would have seen him with the herb."

"Yes, but how would a mere passerby have known he was to take it as a tea that evening?"

"Perhaps the murderer was nearby when the leech gave the merchant his instructions. Besides, if someone wanted Master Gruffydd dead, they had only to see that he had angelica and swap the good herb for the poison. When and how he consumed it would be of little concern to a murderer." Godwin watched as Sidroc headed toward the kitchen with his yield. "Gruffydd never returned home. If there was a switch, it was done at the priory."

"I suppose that narrows the possibilities."

"Not by much. If any of this speculation is true, then the murderer both attended the fair *and* the guild feast. That is practically the entire town!"

Constance was shaking her head again. "It sounds so unlikely, Godwin. Are you certain the leech isn't attempting to cast the blame elsewhere. After all, you found the water hemlock in his booth. It looks as if he made a dreadful mistake and is afraid to admit it."

"Yes, it is the simplest explanation," Godwin agreed, "and the correct one, part of me thinks, and yet . . ." He rested his elbows on his knees. "I'm convinced the water hemlock was harvested no earlier than yesterday. The leech would have had little opportunity to roam the marshes then, hunting herbs, for he was sorely occupied with his trade. True, he could have dug the herb at dawn, before the fair opened, but somehow, I don't believe it."

"I cannot believe Maegden had anything to do with her husband's death," Constance insisted.

"Well it could not have been Asheferth acting alone, because he was not at the guild feast." Reluctantly, Godwin rose from the bench, "I'd better go and speak to her. I'll call on you before I leave Bordweal."

When Godwin arrived a few minutes later at the midwife's toft, he found no one home. A neighbor told him they were all at the fair. When he asked if Maegden was with them, she only shrugged.

He stood in the lane, hands on hips, irritably wondering where the merchant's wife could be—surely not at the fair one day after her husband was poisoned! He scowled across the rolling hills toward Hexham, thinking about his botched proposal to Constance. What a fool! How would he ever mend matters? Not until Fulk was well out of the picture, he realized.

He stalked across the orchard, thinking he would have to hunt down Hafren in order to find Maegden. Rounding the corner of the manor house, his gaze swept over the fields to the dense forest beyond. He stopped. Then, instead of entering the hall, he continued to the stables, where he found Eilaf and Bosa sitting in quiet wonderment near a baby foal. Godwin smiled briefly at the tender sight—boy and man hunkered near the lanky newborn, the mare spent but watchful. He motioned for them to stay as he collected his horse. Once in the lane, he urged Saedraca to a canter.

It did not take him long to reach the path leading to the hermitage. He drew in the horse's reins and cautiously approached the cottage. There was a mount tied nearby. Seeing Saedraca, it reared its head, tossing out a neigh of recognition. Drawing his sword, Godwin strode to the door and banged hard with his hilt. "Open! It is your lord."

He heard a muted curse, footsteps, and a lock turn. When the door was pulled wide, Asheferth glared out with furious eyes. On the couch behind him was Maegden.

Sixteen✿

Godwin hauled his knight from the hermitage, slamming the door closed behind. He briefly glimpsed Maegden's pale face as she cast down her eyes. Wordlessly, Godwin sheathed his sword and motioned for Asheferth to follow. When they were well away from the cottage, Godwin turned on him. "You sicken me, Asheferth. She was widowed last night! Have you no honor?"

Asheferth's sullen eyes turned bewildered. "What has a merchant's death to do with my honor?"

"By God's eyeballs, Asheferth, a man is dead! You have committed adultery! Does that not trouble you? Can you be so callous?"

The knight shrugged and glanced at his horse, as if he yearned to quit this trying scene. "A courtly knight serves true love above all else—"

"For the love of Mary, boy, what are you *saying!* Adultery is no light matter! And now a man is dead! What foul business are you mired in?"

Asheferth stared a moment, and then burst out laughing. "You think I murdered her fat husband?" When the laughter died, his eyes grew hard. "I should have. He deserved to die. I should have run the coward through with my blade." His hand strayed to his hip, but the sword was not there.

Godwin studied him. "You had no part in the merchant's

death? Nor Maegden?"

"No! I won't deny we wished him dead. He was evil! But it was the leech who granted our desire. Maegden said he made a mistake and gave out the wrong herb, or potion, or some such thing." He waved his hand vaguely.

"That's one possibility," Godwin said. "But I'm looking into another. The leech is a learned man, schooled in herbs. He swears he gave Master Gruffydd the *right* herb, that someone switched it for a deadly one."

Asheferth drew himself up. "And you think it was Maegden? But she is a lady—I'd serve no less! She has nobility, I assure you." He earnestly explained, "Her father betrayed her, let a merchant defile his own daughter to line his pockets!"

"I don't care, Asheferth! Don't you see how this looks? You are having an affair with a woman whose husband is now dead, possibly murdered!"

"Pah!" he spat out. "He was a merchant, his enemies legion from what Maegden says. If he was murdered, you'll no doubt find the guilty one, if you probe his dealings but a little." He eyed Godwin. "Yet, maybe justice has been served. Would it not be best to let the matter be?"

Godwin studied him coldly, saying, "You'll stay away from Maegden until I'm satisfied his death was an accident, or find his murderer. Is that understood?"

"I cannot abandon her now when she needs me most! If this is a test of our love, so be it. I'll not betray her."

"Asheferth! Have you no sense? She is newly widowed, in mourning! She cannot see you! If your affair is discovered, the cost for her could be high! Think of Maegden—*her* reputation. In time, it may be that you will be reunited, but her kin and yours will have much to say in the matter."

Godwin watched carefully to see if his words were getting through. Could Asheferth be this ingenuous? "Get your gear and go. I'll see Maegden back to Bordweal."

Inside, they found her sitting demurely on the couch, hands folded, head lowered. Asheferth, casting one more sullen look at Godwin, knelt before her, saying, "My love, we must be parted for a time."

Maegden lifted her face, her shapely lips parted, as if to protest, but she only nodded, saying, "Yes."

"It will be for a short while only, I promise. My lord has commanded it."

Maegden said, "You will tire of waiting and find another."

"Lady, don't say such a thing! I would never find joy with another!"

"Do you promise?"

"I do."

Godwin stood awkwardly by, wishing they would conclude their farewell. But Maegden had come prepared to offer a token of her love, for she pulled a small silver locket from a purse at her belt. "I knew today would be our last so I brought this." She handed it to Asheferth, and Godwin glimpsed a finely crafted ornament. The knight cupped it in his hand as Maegden held up a tiny key on a golden thread. "You may love only the woman who can unlock it." She slipped the key back into her purse.

Asheferth finally rose to move quickly about the cottage, collecting his belongings. Before departing, he knelt before Maegden once more and lifted her hands to brush them against his lips, replacing them gently in her lap. Silently, he left the hermitage. Shortly after, Godwin heard the slow footfalls of his horse. He stood before Maegden and held out a hand. "Come, let us walk a while."

She raised her dark head, showing him chastened eyes. As she stared up, Godwin understood why a man might covet her. Maegden was like a maid from a romance—the sweetly tempting girl who roams the moors and secret woodland dells until a chance meeting unites her with a lover. She was smiling shyly now. Godwin smiled sadly back as he extended his hand. She had learned that a coy look could bring results. It faltered now and faded when she saw Godwin was unaffected.

Once outside, they walked slowly toward one of the many

forest tracts that extended from the hermitage. "You think I'm wanton, lord?" she asked. She spoke disinterestedly with no concern for what his answer might be.

"No."

"A temptress, like Eve?"

"It's not my place to judge you."

"You are the law. Does not the law judge?" When he did not answer, she said, "I love Asheferth."

"You were married."

"Aye, and I wished my master dead. Prayed for it. And my prayers were answered." Again, he made no reply. "I grew to hate him. It did not begin that way, but it became so."

The trail was well trodden, though narrow, beaten to accommodate the width of a single horse. It climbed gently toward to the summit of the river valley, but Godwin halted before they were long into the murky woods. "Did you poison your husband?"

She strolled on a little farther. "Me?" she asked, glancing over her shoulder. "Nay, it was the leech."

"I think it was someone else, someone who wanted your husband dead."

She turned. "If that's so, I would thank him, for I've been set free, like the nightingale. Do you know the story, lord?"

Godwin took her arm, leading her back down the trail. "Was your life with him so terrible?"

She was silent a moment, brow creased, earnestly pondering his question. Finally, she said, "He was careful to put his marks where they could not be seen."

They reached the clearing and Maegden went straight to Godwin's horse. Stroking its neck, she was unafraid, though Saedraca towered over the tiny woman. "I was with child once—that is what my sister told me—but I lost the babe. He was sorry. He did not mean for me to fall."

Godwin suppressed a rising tide of disgust. "Can you think of anyone who may have killed your husband?"

Once again, she considered his question carefully. She was childlike at times, and Godwin recalled Constance's words. "He was not well liked among the merchants. He was arrogant, you know. On occasion, I would recall for him his lowly roots." Her eyes shone with fleeting malice before she lowered them. "Always he made me regret it."

"My husband was proud and vain, an evil combination in a man. I imagine his funeral will draw few mourners." Maegden ran her hand over Saedraca's great flanks. "How I would love my own mount, a spirited horse such as this."

Godwin smiled faintly. "Perhaps one day you will. But not a stallion, surely?"

Her expression was puzzled. "Why not?"

"Well . . ." He was about to say that ladies rode mares, but changed his mind. Maegden was naïve to be sure, but there was more to her, a strength that would ripen with the years. Given the opportunity, she no doubt *would* sit a stallion. He imagined her flying across the moors. "Why not, indeed?"

But for the journey back to Bordweal, she rode in a more conventional fashion on a pillion behind Godwin. Even this thrilled her. Godwin was almost sorry he had to question her further.

He wanted to know about the herb. When had she first seen him with it? Where had he taken it? But Maegden recalled little. "We met him at his booth on opening day. He was acting strangely. My sister noticed, too. His stomach was ailing him again." She remembered the incident with the flowers more clearly. "He gave us each a flower, then we parted. I was happy to be away from him. I tossed away the lily. Cecelia picked it up, but I told her to leave it."

Godwin kept the horse at a slow pace and asked once more about the herb.

"I did not see him again until that evening," she said. Her head was resting on his back, her voice as small as a child's. "It was in the priory kitchen. Hafren and I were bringing in our dishes. We had labored hard over them, for the servants had the day free."

The kitchen had been crowded with folk. She didn't remember seeing her husband with the herb, but she did recall him blustering in Brother Peter's face, giving orders. "I wanted to be away. I wanted Asheferth."

As they drew closer to Bordweal, Godwin told her about the complaint filed at the faircourt by Master Gruffydd. As his widow, how would she like to proceed? On this, she was clear. "I would like it dismissed, lord. I know nothing of the matter, nor this John Longspee, but if there's been grief between them over a business matter, I have no doubt my husband was the source."

Godwin nodded. "Very well, I'll inform the justices." He was also planning to interview Longspee. He wasn't at the guild feast, but he could have bribed a servant to swap the herbs.

"Have you spoken with Edward? The guild will bury your husband, but you must make known his wishes."

She clutched at Godwin's waist. "I care not about the manner of his burial. He burns in hell, I know it. Why should any of us give thought to him now?"

"Because we must, as well you know," Godwin said. When she did not reply, he said in a gentler voice, "What of Gruffydd's kin? They must be told he is dead."

"He has no kin."

Godwin glanced back. "None at all?"

"His birthplace was Flint, but he spoke ill of it, and washed his hands of kin and Welshmen when he came to the north."

"It will be your burden, then, to manage his affairs. Were you accustomed to assisting him? Do you know his trade?"

"Nay, he wanted me to have no part of it, though once I was eager to learn."

Godwin wondered if he ought to find someone to assist her—an officer of the guild, perhaps? Then he realized Hafren and her husband would likely help.

He steered the horse beyond the fields and orchard flanking the manor, depositing her at her sister's croft. "I ask you not to visit my knight, Maegden." She nodded solemnly, like a scolded girl.

Godwin studied her as she crossed the close to disappear into the house, thinking how she freely admitted to wanting Gruffydd dead and for reasons hard to deny. Though it sickened him, a heavy hand in a husband was common enough, yet Gruffydd sounded unusually cruel. He recalled the merchant's maltreated servants and felt a shiver of disgust.

At the manor, he found the household preparing for supper. Though he would have liked to, he could not stay, despite Cynwyse's insistent invitation; duties in Hexham and his mother's ire kept him steadfast in his regrets. He did grant Bosa and Eilaf their wish to remain for the night, for he did not know the state of Dilston Hall, and they were keen on the newborn foal.

Constance walked with him to where he'd left Saedraca tethered. Godwin was relieved to sense their quarrel was behind them. They were, as always, at ease with one another, and he recounted his meeting with Asheferth and Maegden. Her eyebrows lifted when she learned of their tryst in the hermitage, but she let out no shocked exclamations, nor did he expect any. "She denies murder, of course," he said. "But she had reasons besides Asheferth—good ones some might say—to be rid of him." He told her about Gruffydd's evil treatment.

Constance's face became grim. "The poor girl! Yet I still won't believe she had a part in his death."

"There are other possibilities. According to Maegden, he was despised by many for his ruthless business dealings."

They drew up to where the horse stood grazing and stopped to admire the westerly sun as it illuminated the river valley, lighting it from within so that the Tyne sparkled like a silver ribbon wending through green slopes. The vista would only grow lovelier as evening approached, and Godwin yearned to remain. His duties were always taking him from the people he wanted most to be with. Or were his expectations changing? Without thinking he reached for

Constance's hand. She smiled. Again, before he could consider, he bent down and kissed her. Then he quickly seized the horse's reins and sprang into the saddle. When he ventured a look, she was gazing up at him, her eyes bright with surprise and . . . yes, pleasure. Elated, he fumbled his handling of Saedraca, who protested noisily. Constance fumbled, too—over her words—and they said an awkward farewell. Godwin spurred the horse, and when he dared a backward glance, Constance was still in the lane. They raised their arms in a final farewell.

He grinned at his greenness, and, it had to be admitted, for catching her unaware. Making for the bridge with unusual haste, he visualized once more those startled, violet eyes.

Constance found herself standing in the kitchen, though she recalled nothing of the short walk from the lane. "What be the matter?" Cynwyse demanded, eyeing Constance over a heaping plate of peas and bacon. The cook handed the dish to a servant who scurried in from the hall and then out again just as quickly. "Ye look strange, and yer face is red as a cherry." She came over to peer more closely. "Are ye ill?"

"Nay, I'm . . . hungry, I guess."

"Well, come along then, supper's all ready."

But she only picked at the food set before her, rekindling Cynwyse's concern. The cook said nothing, however, only clucked at Constance's plate when the dishes were cleared.

Later, when the washing up was done and the hall back in order, Cynwyse sought her mistress in the garden, enjoying the mild evening. Autumn was not far off, and soon their world would be cold and bleak.

"Ye didn't eat, but ye don't look fevered —yer color's right again," the cook pronounced as she joined Constance for a walk in the rows of herbs. "Yer looking bonny as a posy." She said this as if it were cause for worry, adding, "Why do ye keep grinnin'? Did Lord Godwin give ye some good news?"

"Do I need a reason?" Constance asked irritably. "How do I usually look?"

The cook stooped to pluck a weed. "Oh . . . like ye want no surprises comin' yer way."

"I like surprises!" Constance objected. "At least, I like pleasant surprises. Honestly, Cynwyse, you make me sound like a sour old spinster."

"Now, I said nothing of the kind, lady. Yer a woman with important matters to mind. Of course ye act serious. I just wish ye could have a bit more fun now and then—Ach, will ye look at these bugs on my sage!"

"I danced at the feast the other night."

Cynwyse chuckled. "That ye did, lady!" She was plucking tiny green insects from the herb, holding one up to study it more closely. "Some say ye can eat these, that they taste sweet and ward off colds."

Constance wrinkled her nose. "I would rather have a cold."

"Aye, there are better remedies," Cynwyse agreed, crushing it between her fingers. She turned her curious gaze on Constance. "What *did* Lord Godwin have to say?"

Constance resumed her strolling, randomly plucking stems of sweet-smelling herbs. She added angelica to her bouquet. "We talked mostly of Master Gruffydd."

"Ach, such an evil business! Water hemlock tea! Can ye imagine! I'll wager there's no line to visit the leech now."

"No, his booth has been closed."

"And what of that evil wasp?" Cynwyse asked, her pebble eyes clouding. "Did ye speak of Fulk? Will Lord Godwin deal with him for ye?"

At the mention of Godwin's name, Constance felt her limbs flutter again. "I'm afraid there's nothing Godwin can do—nor I apparently. The matter will be decided by Lord Eilan and the archbishop." There was only a trace of bitterness in her voice.

Cynwyse nodded. "A good man is Lord Eilan. If anyone can stand up to the archbishop, it'll be him." She turned a bleak face to study the horizon. "Still, I feel strange as an onion, lady. Trouble is a-comin'. I've spoken with the saints and made ye a powerful charm, but something tells me it won't be enough."

Constance added sprigs of basil to her spray and held it to her face, inhaling the mingled scents—the smells of summer. Accustomed to Cynwyse's dire forebodings, she said, "I've decided to go to Dunbar."

The cook brightened. "Aye, a good plan, lady. The greater the distance between ye and that plague the better!"

"It should please you to know, then, that he was called from Hexham this morning."

The cook shook her head. "He's an evil tide—soon away and back again. Will Lord Godwin go with us to Dunbar?"

"Nay, he has duties here, Cynwyse, the merchant's death and a fair to deal with."

The cook pulled a face. "Bless my bread, I was forgettin'!"

They reached the last row of herbs, and Cynwyse glared down at a bed of bolted greens, looking disgusted by their frailty in the late summer heat. "We'll set out once Godwin's messenger returns from Dunbar," Constance said, adding borage to her bouquet. The tiny cerulean blooms contrasted pleasingly with the greens.

"The sooner the better to my way of thinking, lady!"

Gazing toward Hexham, Constance was not sure she agreed.

SEVENTEEN ✠

*N*icolette's husband was enraged. He called for three of his henchmen and, after taking up his sword, went straight-away to his wife's chamber. The door was broken down, and when the husband saw the knight, he gave orders to kill the stranger. Yves was unafraid. Quick as lightening, he grabbed a sword from one of his assailants and waited for the others to attack. He was likely to lose the battle, but the knight was deter-mined to maim his attackers if he could, for he wanted nothing more than to die a brave and honorable death before his lady.

The lord studied Yves, and then Nicolette, perceiving that a great love had formed between them. He asked the knight where he came from and how had got there. Yves courteously answered all his questions, and the husband replied, "Let us find this ship, and I will send you back to the sea. I shall be pleased if you are drowned, but if you should survive, your life will be an empty, lonely one, for you will never see my wife again."

The henchmen and the husband captured Yves and put him on the ship. It set sail immediately, and the distraught knight prayed to God never to let him come to a port if he could not regain his Nicolette. But the vessel brought him back to the harbor where he had first boarded, and Yves recognized his native land. Disembarking, he planned to gather some of his fellow knights and take the ship back to the castle where he would wage battle against the lord. But as soon as Yves stepped off the ship, it got under way again, abandoning him with no way to return to his lady.

Yves's friends rejoiced at his return. The knight was highly honored in his land, but through it all he was melancholy, lamenting his lost love. His kin wanted him to take a wife, but he refused, saying he would only marry the lady who could untie his knotted shirt. The news traveled throughout the country, and women came from all over to try their luck, but none could undo the knot.

Meanwhile, Nicolette's husband imprisoned her in a dark tower. Her misery was unbearable, the pain and suffering indescribable. For two years she remained in the tower without a single moment of pleasure. The lady mourned for her lover and for the lingering torture of her confinement. "If I could escape," she said aloud, "I would go to where you put to sea and drown myself." She got up and went to the door. Astonished, Nicolette found that it was unlocked, the guard gone. With no one stopping her, she made her way to the harbor where she found the magic ship. Nicolette boarded it, hoping to find Yves, but no one was there, and the vessel immediately set out, taking her across the sea. . . .

EiGHTEEN✝

As Maegden predicted, Gruffydd's funeral drew few mourners. The officers of the guild were there, along with several of its members, yet as Godwin cast his eyes around the graveside circle, he saw no one, save Fara, who displayed anything in the way of sorrow or regret. The bland-faced widow, flanked by her sister and nieces, was staring absently at the stone wall encircling the priory grounds. Hafren divided her time between keeping the fidgeting girls in line and soothing a sister who was not in distress.

Thick clouds had rolled in during the night, the first drops spilling at dawn. They came lightly now as a fine mist, but the darkly laden sky threatened to spill its burden at any moment. Brother Elias, sensing they would be drenched momentarily, hastened through the litany, sprinkling holy water and incensing with adroit speed. The canons began shoveling dirt before the final amen was spoken, prompting folk to quickly throw down their tokens. Most turned away even before the mementos came to rest on the stout coffin now deep in the earth.

Brother Elias and the canons led the mourners in a loose procession to the cathedral. They walked with slow dignity while the impending downpour was held in check, but when fat drops began to fall, decorum was abandoned and the mourners made a dash for the north entrance.

Fara remained, pulling a shawl over her head as she laid a sprig of herbs on the grave. Godwin waited, and together they walked to the church. The funeral feast would be held in the Refectory and hosted by the guild, but Godwin would depart before the service proceeded that far. He had fair business to mind, writs to address, a host of small tasks that had been neglected these past days.

Stepping inside the cathedral's dark interior, they shook the rain from their capes. As Fara and the others moved across the cathedral toward the east door, Godwin signaled to Brother Elias. The acting prior joined him, then glanced in Maegden's direction."

Godwin followed his gaze. Maegden and Hafren walked side by side, the widow smiling happily as she cradled the midwife's youngest in her arms. Her other nieces skipped merrily behind, their mother turning often to shush them, but with little effect, for the echoes of their high, tinkling laughter enchanted them, and the cathedral rang faintly to life with their music.

Brother Elias smiled benevolently. "My bishop would not approve," he said, "but does it not sound like the voices of angels? Children are the greatest blessing."

"Indeed," Godwin said, though he imagined there were times when Hafren did not agree. "And my nephew, brother? Is he one such blessing?"

"He's perfect!" When Godwin cocked a brow, he added, "Of course, he's a boy, so naturally there will be pranks."

"Pranks?" Godwin said, his smile faltering.

"Oh, they are not aimed at me, lord. During our lessons, Eilaf is faultless. It is the canons—they began the mischief."

"What sort of tomfoolery is my nephew into so soon?"

"They act as youths themselves," Brother Elias lamented, contemplating his unruly flock.

"What games do they play with Eilaf?" Godwin asked, growing alarmed.

"Worry not, lord. Your nephew is under my watchful gaze

always. He has a bit of fun now and then—locking a brother in the privy—that sort of thing, but so he should, for he is a diligent pupil."

"You are very forgiving," Godwin said, shaking his head. "Why am I such a nursemaid with my nephew?"

When Godwin returned to the Moot Hall, Burchard was waiting inside with John Longspee. He dismissed the knight and motioned for the other to take a seat. The man quickly obeyed, perching on a bench to gaze wide-eyed around the hall, looking every bit the yeoman farmer awed by the city.

John Longspee was a large man with a pitted, sunburned face, and hands the size of Bosa's. Godwin first informed him that Master Gruffydd's widow had withdrawn the complaint against him. The man let out a whistle of relief, brushing his overgrown hair from a broad forehead. "Thank the Virgin. I was not sure how I would pay the justices their fee."

"Tell me about the dispute between you and Master Gruffydd."

Longspee's face darkened. "A dirty dealin' thief he is— was, I should say." He quickly crossed himself, adding, "Tried to *steal* my wool, not buy it!"

"How?"

"A year's worth of hard work and he offers a few pennies!"

"If that's so, why take his offer?"

"I didn't! It was my wife. I was out moving stock when he paid a call." Longspee touched the side of his head with a paw-like hand. "She fell down a well last year and has not been the same. Not daft, or anything," he assured Godwin, "but scared like a rabbit.

"Anyhow, this merchant comes along and wants my whole bundle for a song! Peddlers always show up this time a year. They know most farmers cannot sell at the fair, with stock and family to mind, so they come to us hoping to buy cheap. We know they do not pay what our wool is worth, but we get a fair enough price. We're no fools! We know the value of our goods!

"But Master Gruffydd, he tells my wife the price has fallen, that it's the best he can offer. Better take it, he says, or we would be stuck with the wool. My wife knows it's not enough, tells him to wait for me. He says take it or leave it, he's moving on. My wife gets nervous and takes the offer. He had a paper ready and she made her mark. He gave her the money and said he'd be back for the wool before the fair."

Godwin shook his head. Gruffydd had indeed been ruthless.

"Of course I wasn't going to take his deal. I would sell my wool to an honest merchant, not a robber! But I knew I had to get the money back to Master Gruffydd first, or it wouldn't be right. Only he sends a henchman instead of coming himself for the wool, and not until two days before the fair! I sent the man away with the merchant's pittance, then had to come myself to sell the wool, even though I'm scared to death about leaving my wife on the farm. But if I hadn't, we'd have starved come winter. And when I saw Master Gruffydd at the fair, he about strangled me! But it was *me* who ought to have done the strangling!" His big hands flexed. "I can't say I'm sorry he's dead."

By the time Godwin showed Longspee from the Moot Hall, the rain was coming down hard. About to close the door, he noticed the leech standing in the Market Square, sheltering beneath one of the stalls used on market days. Sodden, the leech haled Godwin, who waved him over, hustling the bedraggled man inside. Pointing to pegs on the wall where he could hang his dripping cloak, Godwin went over to pour them each some wine and then stirred the fire to life.

The rain beat on the roof like a shower of stone. Godwin was sorry for the fair goers and the merchants, for foul weather meant bad business. Cracking open the door, he peered outside, marveling at the fog of rain. Pools were forming in the cobbled pavement. Across the square, Gruffydd's house was darkly shuttered, and he wondered if the servants Emma and Malcolm were inside. "It won't let up for some time," he said, closing the door. "Unusual for this time of year."

The leech, his thick brows dripping, commented, "If we counted up all the days of strange weather in a year, we might find there's no such thing as *usual* weather—not in the north anyway."

"I expect you're right," Godwin said, taking up his wine. The healer did likewise, his hand shaking badly.

"I'd like to move on," the leech said, coming quickly to his business. "There is no point in remaining if I cannot sell my cures. Do I have your permission to leave Hexham?"

"I'd prefer it if you could stay."

The leech shrugged. "Very well. But word has gone 'round that I poisoned a customer. I'm not exactly welcome in your town."

Godwin, refilling their cups, turned sharply. "Have you been molested?"

"Nay, your cross deputy has been keeping an eye out."

Sitting down again, Godwin marveled at the frail man who thought nothing of taking to the road alone. He must be short on silver, too, with his booth closed. "Do you not fear robbers, traveling alone as you do?"

"Until recently, I had a companion, a boy dear to me." The leech stared across the hall. "At our last halt he fell in love with a serving girl and could not be parted from her." He paused to drain his cup, meeting the bailiff's eyes. "Is not love pitiless? It divides and enslaves."

Godwin raised his brows. "Perhaps. Yet the minstrels tell us that love also ennobles and inspires."

"And what does your own experience tell you?"

Godwin would not be drawn in, saying instead, "Come take your ease at Dilston before returning to the road. It might be that I can find you a traveling companion."

"A generous offer, lord, but you owe me nothing. You are not responsible for my ill fortune."

But Godwin did feel responsible, for if the man was innocent of poisoning the merchant, then it was his duty to prove it.

"You are still of two minds I see," the leech said, nodding as if he sympathized. "On the one hand, there is the simple explanation with proof to back it up—the doddering healer who made a terrible error."

Yes, and on the other hand, Godwin thought, there was a ruthless merchant, his beaten wife and her lover, a flimsy padlock, a full moon, and a bit of moist soil. Not evidence, only stray bits of information that kept him wondering. . . .

"The widow and her lover—you've ruled out their complicity?"

Godwin gazed at the leech, not inclined to answer, so he was surprised when he heard himself say, "Yes, but for reasons not rational." The leech nodded again, and Godwin stood up restlessly, moving toward the wine jug before changing his mind and returning to the bench. "The lover is a knight who would not kill without a challenge, and certainly not by poison. The widow had a score of reasons to murder her husband, but denies any guilt, and I believe her." He shook his head. "I've found many who did not love the merchant, had cause to hate him even, but none is a murderer, unless I'm a fool!"

"Killers among ordinary folk are rare. Either they are easy to mark or nearly impossible."

Godwin said, "I've seen men hewn to pieces by the sword and beaten down by charging horses. Once I saw a man beg for mercy even as his head rolled to the earth. But that is war, a wretched business made tolerable, honorable even, by church and king. But murder—a sly and secret killing—*is* a rare thing in my experience. It is easy to commit, yet an uncommon act."

"Oh, yes, easy indeed," the leech agreed. "Taking a life is not so difficult, requiring only a bit of strong cord, a torch held close to a house, a poisonous plant. The burden comes later in living with the weight of committing the worst evil. Killers are those who do not fear the burden, or are so accustomed to death that it has been rendered commonplace."

They waited for the rain to subside before setting out for Dilston Hall. The leech needed little more encouragement to accept Godwin's offer of hospitality and agreed to meet the bailiff where the east road joins Hexham. He had only to fetch his pony from the stable—it was already laden with his books and gear—and pay the stable boy his penny for keeping watch.

Godwin used the time to check on Emma and Malcolm. And a good thing it was, for he found them living off dwindling stores. The dark house was exactly as it had been, as if Maegden had never returned. "Where's your mistress? Surely you've not been on your own these past days?"

Emma told him that Maegden had come only once to say she was giving the house and all its contents to the priory, that they could stay on until they found other work, or until St. Andrews took possession.

"Have you found other service?" When they shook their heads, he asked, "Where are your kin?" Malcolm started to reply, but a warning glance from Emma made him stop. Godwin guessed they were runaways and pressed them no further, saying, "Well, you can't stay here."

Thus, when Godwin met the leech at the east road, he came with two more in tow. He had borrowed a pony to bear them and their possessions, though the children were so scrawny, their goods so scarce, Saedraca could easily have accommodated them all. Yet Emma was still nervous with Godwin. When he helped her on the pony, she recoiled. Malcolm did not show the same fear, only a wariness rarely seen in one so young.

However, they perked up during the journey to Dilston,

not bothered by the light rain that pattered gently on their worn smocks. Godwin and the leech smiled, watching as they craned to see everything along the path—the tops of great trees, a songbird in a holly bush, a fluttering moth.

Duff came out to greet the party as it drew up in the croft, clucking his tongue when he saw Emma and Malcolm. "More servants, lord? Bless me, Dilston's bursting with 'em!" Then he turned, held two bony fingers to his mouth and whistled—a screech that made Emma jump.

"Find some quarters will you, Duff? I'll keep them with me for now." Dismounting, Godwin handed the reins to the stable boy who came trotting to the steward's summons. Gesturing to the leech, he said, "Duff, we have a guest, a learned healer. Can you help him get settled?" Addressing the leech, Godwin added, "When you are rested, come to the hall. You'll find food and company if you've an appetite for them."

Godwin took Emma and Malcolm to the kitchens at the rear of the rambling manor house. He was still adjusting to the scouring and polish all the rooms had been subjected to. His beloved hall seemed larger now, the sounds less muffled, as if the years of accumulated dust and smoke—now scrubbed away—had occupied considerable space. After introducing the sister and brother to the cook, he told them to eat their fill, and he would fetch them shortly. Next he went to find his mother.

She was alone in a small chamber off the hall where the girls did their sewing. A parchment lay in her lap, and from the ink stains on her fingers and pensive stare, he surmised she was composing a poem. "Oh, my son!" she cried as he came into the room. "How timely —hark!"

I sing this song most sad,
About a life gone bad,
Ever suffering betrayal,
In exile I weep.

She recited the grim lines with a dramatic intonation. "A bit depressing, Mother," he said. "I like the one about the missing shoe better." He bent down to kiss her cheek and then pulled a stool close. "Besides, what do you know of betrayal and exile? You've led a charmed life."

"There is more to me than you know, my impertinent son." Her eyes dropped to the words she had scratched. "I've borne my share of hardship—not the trials of a warrior, to be sure, but the unsung hurts of a wife and mother."

Godwin frowned, for his mother was not prone to introspection. "Of course you have, Mother."

Gunnilda raised her eyes, and they teased when she said, "One of my greatest sorrows is this empty house! Filled with my grandchildren it ought to be!" When she saw his expression, she hastened to add, "Very well! I'll say no more on the subject!"

"Good! But while we're on the topic of children, I've a favor to ask." Godwin told his mother about Emma and Malcolm. "Would you take them into service? I'm concerned about the girl. She's wary of men, and this house is crowded with them. And I don't want to divide these children. Something tells me they have dealt with great hardship."

"What am I? A convent?" she protested. Yet there was sympathy in her eyes, and Godwin knew she would agree. "Is she pretty? I like my girls pretty, you know."

"She is lovely. And the boy's quite likable, good with a pony and ready for larger. They need a bit of fattening up is all."

One of the hounds burst into the room, panting furiously, as if he had been searching high and low for his master. His great tail pummeled the air and anything in its wide path as he greeted Godwin.

"Muddy paws!" Gunnilda cried. "Look at the floor! And they were just mopped!"

"It's raining, Mother. What do you expect?" The dog was trying to lick his face, and the more Godwin leaned away, the harder the dog tried to climb into his lap to reach it.

Duff poked his head into the room. "A messenger has just arrived from Dunbar, my lord and lady. He is waiting in the hall."

Godwin rose from the stool and then helped his mother. The parchment slid from her lap, forgotten. When they entered the hall, Godwin knew the tidings were grave, for his messenger's tired eyes slid away as Godwin searched his face. Then he marshaled, straightening to deliver his message with dignity. "Lord Godwin, Lady Gunnilda, I regret to say that Lord Eilan is dead."

Nineteen ✠

They would make a large company, ensuring a safe journey. These were Godwin's words to Constance, said after he had delivered the news of Lord Eilan's death. Their tentative intimacy receded as they spoke of the great man's passing and quietly made plans for the journey. Though his barony was in Northumbria, his widow Galiena wished Eilan to be buried with her kin in Dunbar.

It was decided that Constance and Gunnilda would set out together. Cynwyse would make the journey too, along with Bosa, Eilaf, and Gunnilda's steward, Duff. A servant would drive the wagon. They would go escorted by four knights, led by William the Welshman. Godwin could not leave immediately, for their departure coincided with the last day of Hexham's fair. But their entourage would not be a speedy one, halting two nights before reaching Dunbar, and he promised to join them on the road.

At first light they departed. It was a token sunrise, the sky a vast gray sheet, adding to the bleak mood of the travelers. As they climbed the slopes of the dale to a clearing in its upland forests, Constance turned to survey the valley that had become her home. Her spirits lifted a little as she studied the broad combe with its alternating slopes of dense woodland and neatly plowed terraces. The priory cathedral gleamed in the dull light, the Tyne lapping at its feet and wearing a fringe of tangled, green growth. Looking east, she saw a buttery strip on the horizon promising fair skies by late morning.

Yet when she turned to face the road again, her sorrow lurched back like a blow. She urged her mare ahead, not wanting the others to see her grief. The tears kept coming, and when she steadied herself, they came yet again. All that she delighted in—the valley, the quiet spell of the forest, the ancient oaks like sentinels—starkly reminded her that Lord Eilan would never again enjoy such pleasures.

Gunnilda, staring blankly ahead, rode in silence. Wrapped in a shroud-like mantle, she went flanked by Eilaf, Bosa, and Duff. Next came the baggage cart and behind rode the watchful knights. Constance's own steward did not accompany her, for Hereberht had another errand, one that took him south to the court of England's regent, Hubert de Burgh. On the previous day, in the midst of her worst sorrow, he had approached Constance, as gently as he was capable, saying, "The death of Lord Eilan, my lady, complicates the issue of your suitor, Fulk de Oilly."

She had wanted to protest, to say that such considerations were selfish, that her mind was dwelling only on the tragic loss of a great man and father. Yet it had shamed her to realize she could not object, for she *had* wondered about her fate after Godwin delivered the news. And so she had waited with guilty anticipation to hear what her steward might say.

"Lord Eilan's barony will now pass to your son. Lord Eilan's lord is now his."

Lord Eilan's lord? Constance had never thought of her father-in-law as a vassal, but of course he was.

"As your son's guardian, you hold from the crown now. Your lord is England's regent."

"The crown," she murmured.

"I have a plan, lady."

It was a good plan; and for the first time since Fulk's coming, Constance felt she might thwart him *and* on her terms.

She had instructed Hereberht to use all means—her entire dowry if necessary—to win their goal. If more was needed, he was to pledge it. She would raise the silver somehow—sell her possessions, whatever was required.

It was not long before the party passed into the Marches, to wide, scrubby wastes where the wind never rests. Sunshine came, as promised, but it offered little warmth in the persistent gusts. There was no chatter among the company as they held tightly to their cloaks, plodding slowly toward Jedburgh Abbey where they would halt for the night.

But beyond the dreary landscape of the Roman Wall, the terrain began to change. The lonely border moorland slowly gave way to thickets and sapling groves, and to softly curving hillocks dressed in wide stretches of woodland. Bosa and Eilaf spurred ahead to race along the road built straight and true by the Romans. Their presence was strong in these hills, for their earthworks could still be seen. As the party drew alongside the River Rede, Cynwyse suggested they halt for a meal, glancing around for an inviting spot to settle.

They did not dwell after their supper, however, for they must arrive at the abbey well before eventide. Duff and the knights did not need to remind them that these empty hills were no place to be found after nightfall.

The road continued to follow the course of the river, flanked by slopes that climbed ever steeper and higher as they journeyed north. The forest grew dense. Constance remarked on an impressive peak in the distance, and Duff chuckled, saying it was a trifling compared to the lofty marvels his Scotland had to offer.

Under other circumstances, Constance would have taken pleasure in the discovery of new country, but the farther from Bordweal she traveled, the uneasier she became. She told herself it was the shock of Eilan's death—so sudden and tragic. It brought both sadness and unease—a reminder that life can take a sudden vicious turn. Yet as her discomfort grew, she could not help feeling that her disquiet betokened something more.

Cynwyse was no help. Riding alongside Constance, she was still feeling "strange as an onion." She muttered and peered darkly up narrow clefts and into deeply shadowed woodland. Constance's agitation grew, aggravated by the silent forest and loud groaning of the baggage cart as it lumbered over the uneven road. Eventually, she could think of nothing but her desire to turn back for home.

Arriving at a fork in the road, the party bore right. Duff told her they were now following the Jed Water, that the abbey wasn't far. The road twisted with the river's bends and the steep hills lessened. Now and then they saw a cottage and folk working small gardens. Then, coming around a wide sloping curve, Jedburgh Abbey lay stretched before them.

It was a small abbey, a jewel glowing warmly in the afternoon light. The monastery's cathedral sat perched above the river, its buildings and houses cascading down the hillside almost to the banks. The sight heartened Constance, her anxiety slipping away as they drew closer to its burnished walls and arcades. They went to the gatehouse where a solemn canon greeted them. Gunnilda was a frequent guest and their arrival had been anticipated. Shortly, a servant was leading the travelers through the silent grounds to the guest rooms.

Constance was struck by the contrast between Hexham's priory cathedral and this one. St. Andrews was grander, but unkempt compared to the carefully tended Jedburgh Abbey. The canons here were gravely serene, infusing the place with a contemplative peacefulness. She found herself looking forward to the Vesper hymns.

Evensong did not disappoint. After they were settled, Constance, Gunnilda, and Cynwyse made their way back to the cathedral just as the pure voices of the choir began to sing. Later, when Constance lay down for the night, the Song of Mary echoed in her ears.

* * *

In the morning, she arose early to attend Lauds, praying long for Lord Eilan. After a small breakfast, they took to the road once more, bearing northeast toward the sea and Berwick where they would pass another night. By midday tomorrow, she was told by Duff, they would arrive at Dunbar.

Gunnilda, in a reflective mood, was more eager to talk today. She rode in front with Constance, recalling stories of her sister and Lord Eilan, her dead husband, and their early days at Earl Patric's court.

Gunnilda and her sister Galiena, Constance's mother-in-law, had both wed small but worthy northern barons. Yet they kept strong ties with kin, especially their brother, the earl. Aidan and Godwin had done their knightly training at Dunbar, and the sisters were frequent visitors to its court. Reaching way into her past, she recounted stories of their travels, battles, and sorrows.

By midmorning, the party was passing Calkou Abbey on the Tweed. It was a splendid church, and Constance wanted to stop, but Gunnilda declined, for they still had a great distance to travel through the Tweed Valley. Settlements were thick about the abbey, but tapered off the farther they traveled from it. Soon, they were riding along a narrow tract, muddy from the recent rains and edged by dense woodland. Nearby, the river raced in its banks. The sky above was bright, the day already warm, and Constance was happy for the woodland, enveloping them like a cool blanket.

Gunnilda spurred her horse, motioning for Constance to do likewise and soon they were well in front of the others. Both William the Welshman and Duff shouted for them to wait, and when Constance glanced back, she saw the cart was having trouble negotiating the sloppy road. Gunnilda waved a dismissive hand and leaned over to say, "Did you know Eilan loved *me* first?" She laughed at Constance's expression. "Does that surprise you, dear?" They rode on, but slowly. "I begged my father to let us wed, but I was already promised to Aluric. The bond had been made; it could not be undone."

Constance was still digesting the revelation. Lord Eilan and Gunnilda in love? "So you married Aluric," she said, "though you loved Eilan?"

"Yes," she sighed. "It was my father's will."

"And Lord Eilan married your sister?"

"Yes."

"Did it not wound you to see them together?"

"Oh, yes, it was difficult," Gunnilda said. "And for Eilan, too—I could tell. Yet we were near one another, that was something. Then the babies started coming . . ." She gave a little shrug.

Constance stole a glance, trying to find a lovesick girl in the woman riding beside her. "Did you . . . grow fond of Godwin's father?"

She thought a moment, and then said, "We kept each other well. I worked hard at rearing, he at lordship. We were content."

"You never remarried," Constance observed.

"No. Offers came—I was still lovely you know. But I wished to remain a widow and my brother abided my will. And so I have."

"If he had pressed a husband on you, would you have conceded?"

"Of course." She glanced at Constance, thin eyebrows raised high. "And perhaps he should have. Women are not meant to be alone, unless they desire the cloister. More often than not, the man chosen becomes dear. We fashion happiness from what is dealt."

"What if the man chosen is unworthy? Or . . . what if the woman loves another?"

"As I loved Eilan?"

Suddenly, they heard a shriek from Cynwyse. Constance pulled up on her reins, wheeling the horse around. She saw four mounted men bearing down on the party, riding from the woods. Flying across the verge with swords raised, they took up a position on the road, separating Constance and

Gunnilda from their company.

Godwin's knights drew their swords, forming a phalanx before Bosa, Eilaf, Duff, and the servant, but Constance and Gunnilda were cut off from their protection. When the lines were drawn up, swords pointing, William the Welshman shouted, "This party travels with few goods. There is naught to rob but our food. If you would have it, take it and be off. Leave us in peace, and we'll not molest you."

But Constance did not think these men were common highwaymen. They acted more like soldiers, grim and steady. One of the attackers, the leader she guessed, shouted, "We'll soon take what we want. Keep your heads and do as I ask, and *we* shall not molest *you!*"

A movement in the woods caught Constance's eye. From farther down the road, another mounted man emerged slowly from the forest, unseen by her companions, except Gunnilda. Constance glanced sharply at her, but she shook her head and Constance guessed her mind. If they tried to warn their knights, they might be distracted, making them vulnerable.

The two sides continued to face each other, swords out, reins drawn tight. The horses snorted fiercely, sensing battle, pawing the wet earth. For Constance it was unbearable, watching as the lone man worked his way stealthily toward the company, whose attention was fastened solely on the armed bandits before them. Finally, she could stand it no longer, for he was coming up fast on Eilaf. She screamed the boy's name just as the man swiftly dismounted and dragged him from the saddle.

Godwin's knights wheeled around, but it was too late. Eilaf was held tightly against his captor's chest, a knife at his throat. Bosa cried out, jumping from his horse, but the leader shouted, "Stay, and the boy will not be harmed!" freezing the deputy in his tracks.

William the Welshman's lips twisted into a sneer. "A ransom is what you seek, then? Very well, you shall have it. But I warn you, keep the boy safe, or the man who hunts you will not rest until you are all dead!"

"No!" Constance shouted. Two of the attackers glanced her way, though they kept their swords trained on the knights. "If it is a ransom you seek, take me and leave the boy."

The leader, never taking his eyes from William, said, "Perhaps we will take you both." He risked a swift look and seeing her dismay, laughed. "I jest! We are honorable men, not highway thugs. You may take the boy's place, but I warn you, the ransom had better be equal or greater. Now come!"

"No, lady!" Cynwyse wailed. But Constance dismounted. Beside her, Gunnilda sobbed, and Constance reached up to briefly clasp her hand. The leader shouted, "Hurry!" and she went over to stand beside his mount. He sheathed his sword and plucked her from the ground. Positioning her in front, he clamped his arm around her waist. Then he motioned to the man holding Eilaf, and the boy was released. When he rejoined his comrades, the leader said to William the Welshman, "Follow us and we kill her."

"What's your demand? Where should it be sent?" William shouted as the attackers wheeled around their horses.

The leader shouted, "It shall soon be made known." With that, they spurred hard and thundered off. Constance twisted her head to glimpse a last look at her companions. No one had moved. Gunnilda sat slumped in her saddle, weeping. Cynwyse was frantically calling to her. William the Welshman was studying the abductors as they galloped away. Then, all was cut off from her view as the horse passed around a bend.

Panic welled up. She knew stories of seizures, of folk never again seen by their kin. Oh God, what had she done! Aldwin! She fought to control the terror, telling herself they only wanted silver. When they had it, she would be set free. The man's arm tightened around her as they sped around another curve in the road, the horses leaving churned-up mud in their wakes.

At least they would not be difficult to track, she thought,

regaining her composure. She recalled William's steady scrutiny. He would report every detail to the one who would not stop until she was recovered. Godwin would find her, she was sure. And she ought to help by learning all she could. "Who are you and where are you taking me?" she shouted over the din of galloping horses. The leader did not answer or even acknowledge her words. Every few minutes he glanced over his shoulder.

He had a short dark beard, olive skin, and black eyes— like a Saracen, or how she imagined one might look. They all wore helms and mail hauberks beneath black surcoats devoid of blazons or devices. They carried themselves like seasoned soldiers.

On they went at a breakneck pace until Constance felt as trammeled as the road. Suddenly, the Saracen pulled up sharply on his reins, bringing the horse to a halt so abrupt the wind was knocked from her. They were at another fork. The leader gestured for his men to bear northeast upon the main road. "Ride hard!" he commanded. They sped off, leaving Constance alone with the Saracen.

He got down from the horse, taking the reins. Tugging the beast along, he quickly doubled back a ways. Then, just before the fork, he led the horse off the road to the rocky margin alongside the forest. Clinging to the saddle, Constance's calm began to crumble as she waited to see what this new development would bring. Was he taking her into the woods? If so, why?

But they did not go into the forest. When once again they came to the fork, he quickly led the horse up the smaller, narrower branch, still keeping off the road. Every few moments, he glanced over his shoulder.

Finally, Constance understood. Anyone pursuing would naturally follow the well marked trail of horses on the main road. No one would see that one had turned up the other road, especially when there were no hoof marks in the mud. No one would be rescuing her. She must either save herself or wait to see how the ransom played out.

She stared balefully at the Saracen's back, thinking that if she could get the reins, she might escape. But he kept a tight grip on them, and a careful eye on her. After a league or so, he led the horse back to the road. Within moments, they were flying again, the Saracen spurring the horse mercilessly.

Steadily they climbed from the Tweed Valley. Gradually the woods thinned and the steep grade leveled to rolling plains of gorse and bracken. Without pause or rest, they continued, passing no settlements. There was no one she could shout to for help, though it was unlikely any villain or freeholder would challenge her captor. By her reckoning, they were bearing northwesterly, but there was nothing else of use to note in the barren terrain. Then, on the horizon, a knot of woodland showed itself, rising from a cluster of solitary hills. As they drew closer, she saw a small castle perched on the highest rise.

It became apparent that a great battle had once visited it and the surrounding land. They rode past burned-out crofts and barns, their remains overrun with weedy grasses. The Saracen finally checked his horse, the poor beast dripping froth, its flanks glistening. He dropped his arm from her waist, for where could she run even if she managed to escape? He made for the fortification, its walls blackened by fire, battlements crumbling. "Why do you take me to a ruin? How long will you keep me?" As before, he ignored her.

The land surrounding the castle was sparsely wooded. Many great trees had been hewn to fuel the siege, or so she guessed. Their jagged stumps littered the woods like huge broken teeth. The only sounds were the even footfalls of the horse and the soft chinking of the Saracen's armor. Even the birds had deserted this place.

As they approached the gatehouse, she saw signs of repair. The portcullis was in working order. When they had ridden through, the Saracen leapt down to slide the bolt home. Then he pulled a heavy door closed behind it, hefting a brace securely into place.

Constance gazed at the deserted bailey. It was still paved,

but the flagstones were obscured by grass and scattered debris. The leader dropped the reins, and the horse lowered his head to graze. He motioned for Constance to climb down, offering no assistance, and then led her across the wide enclosure to an open stairway in the northwest corner. Flanking the inner wall were service rooms and accommodations, looking now like burned-out caves and animal dens. At the foot of the stairs he gestured for Constance to ascend.

The stone steps were treacherously uneven, by design no doubt, for it was common to fashion them thusly to slow an assault, or trip a thief in the night. She went carefully, clutching the folds of her gown, the Saracen following closely. Halfway up, a stair began to crumble beneath her foot, and his hand shot out to steady her.

At the landing, they turned down a long covered corridor. At its end, a scarred door met them. He pushed it open and stepped aside, waiting for her to enter. She saw that someone had tried, in vain, to make the room presentable. There were woven fabrics covering its damp walls, new rushes on the floor, and a clean coverlet over a small bed.

When Constance remained motionless on the threshold—for why should she go like a meek calf—he grabbed her arm and pulled her in. "You've shown wisdom today, lady. Do not be wayward now. There are fouler rooms than this in which to keep you." He closed the door and went around lighting candles. "When will you send for the ransom?" she asked. But he only smiled and backed out of the room.

It was a small chamber with a high ceiling and one tiny window looking west. Going over to it, she saw that the sun was low in the sky. Staring at the dusky crimson band on the horizon, Constance prayed, and found she was repeating, not the Virgin's name, but Godwin's.

Turning back to face the room, she saw a fire had been kindled in a small grate. Not for warmth, she guessed, for there was no chill, but to override the smell of mold and grime. She could hear the delicate scratching of mice beneath the bed. There was also a bench and table covered with a cloth, set with bread, cheese, and wine. One corner of the room had been curtained off for a privy.

To keep panic at bay, she occupied herself with washing up. Then she nibbled at the bread, noticing that the mice had been there first. Unable to sit or rest, her mind kept churning out questions. How long would she be kept here? Who had taken her—the Saracen? Or did another employ him? Was he her only guard?

As evening pressed and the light grew dimmer, she added wood to the fire. The room was overly warm, but she welcomed the light. She doused two candles to save them for the coming night.

Finally, she settled on a bench, exhausted and numb. Leaning against the fabric covered wall, she dozed, jerking awake every few minutes. The sky outside was lit with stars when she was awakened suddenly by the sliding bolt. Constance jumped as the door swung open.

There in the doorway, smiling, was Fulk.

TWENTY ✝

"They've gone, lord," Wulfstan said.

"What do you mean 'they've gone'? Gone where?" Godwin asked impatiently. They were in the Moot Hall, and he was eager to be away. Already, it was an hour past sunrise.

Wulfstan shrugged. "To his kin in the south? That's the direction they went. They made no secret of it, and the woman was riding the priory's wild mare—the one gifted to it by the crusader."

Despite the news, Godwin's lips twitched to see his two-fisted deputy's prim outrage. Then he sighed. "Well, they must be brought back."

Yet he hesitated to give the order. After all, he had not accused them of anything, save poor judgment, and he was all but convinced they had nothing to do with Gruffydd's death. Godwin had ordered Asheferth to stay away from Maegden, but his disobedience was no crime. Strictly speaking, the man was still bound to Godwin until released, but he was not inclined to enforce his rights as lord; life would certainly be easier without the unpopular knight disrupting his household. And Maegden? Her actions might displease her parents, but that was no concern of his. Besides, he could always find them if it proved necessary. Godwin knew Asheferth's father well, had taken the boy into service as a favor.

"Shall I fetch them back, lord?" Wulfstan asked. His

mouth tightened when Godwin shook his head. "Word is out they are lovers," he protested. "People are saying they bribed the leech to poison Master Gruffydd. Will you let them get away?"

"I'm not interested in what folk are saying, nor should you be. If the town is against them, then perhaps it's best they are away."

Wulfstan glared, but offered no more objections. They frequently disagreed, but his deputy seldom let his thoughts run contrary to Godwin's for very long. It was loyalty, to be sure, but also an aversion to independent thinking that served them both well.

"I'm off then. Remember, I am but two days away. Send word if you need me." He was fussing and knew it, but could not seem to help himself. Wulfstan took no offense, rubbing his whiskers thoughtfully.

"Well? What's bothering you now?"

His deputy frowned. "First the merchant's death looked to be an accident. Then you thought it might be murder. But if the leech did not do it," he said, extending one finger. "Or the widow and Asheferth." Two more fingers went up. "Who was it?" he asked, gazing at the three fingers.

"I've no idea, Wulfstan."

And yet you go to Dunbar. It seemed a logical retort, but his deputy only nodded, saying, "If new tidings come while you're away, should I act?"

Godwin opened his mouth to say no, but changed his mind. "You are bailiff while I'm gone. Do as you think best."

On his way to the stable, he stopped briefly to see Brother Elias, finding him once more pouring over deeds in his private chamber. He did not seem surprised to see Godwin, though they had said their farewells the previous evening. "My knight and Maegden have left Hexham," he said, coming straight to the point. "She was seen riding the priory's mare."

Brother Elias was slow to reply. "It no longer belongs to

the priory, lord," he said meekly. "She is its rightful owner."

Godwin waited, and in the silence Brother Elias fidgeted with the corner of a parchment, rolling it tightly. "She has given all the merchant's possessions to St. Andrews to be used as alms. She wants nothing in return, yet the white mare captured her heart, so I gave it to her." He looked up. "It seemed fitting, with all the girl's been through." He ducked his head again.

Godwin did not think Brother Elias was referring to the murder of Maegden's husband when he spoke of her trials. He thought he understood, for here was Maegden's confessor. It was likely she had confided in him the brutal reality of her marriage. Had he counseled her? Godwin felt a rush of sympathy for the man, sorry for the burdens he must bear. Brother Elias knew more about Hexham's folk than any. "Well, they have left," Godwin said. "They were seen heading south, she upon the mare."

Brother Elias smiled faintly and Godwin with him. "I can assure you, lord, she played no part in the death of her husband."

Godwin studied the acting prior. Had someone confessed the crime? But of course, he could not ask.

Finally, Godwin fetched Saedraca and crossed the bridge out of town. But as eager as he was to be away, he had one more stop to make before leaving the shire. He was going in that direction anyway and wanted to make sure that Hafren knew of her sister's departure. No doubt she did, but he had to make certain.

The wary look Hafren gave him as he came down the lane toward her croft told Godwin she knew. The midwife, stooping in her garden, straightened slowly as he tied his horse to the gatepost. Her girls were tending the hens—gathering eggs and dung, and spreading feed. With Hafren was another woman with a babe in her arms. This must be the new mother Constance mentioned, Agnes, the one they had come close to losing. She looked well now, though pale in the bright sun. And thoroughly enchanted by her son. Agnes barely glanced up from the babe as he approached, cooing and swaying as she stood near the midwife.

Yes, Hafren told him, she knew that Maegden was gone. "I'll miss her sorely, but she will be happy now. You will not make her return?"

Agnes put the baby to her shoulder, patting his back gently. When she saw Godwin watching, she turned so he could admire the tiny face. He smiled, seeing the baby's fat cheeks and tightly closed eyes. Then it belched, sending forth a stream of white froth. Godwin's smile faltered and he glanced quickly at the women, but they found the babe's actions agreeable, even praised him.

"No," he said, eyeing the sour-smelling stain on Agnes's smock. "I'll leave them for now, but I can't promise it will always be so."

Hafren nodded, wiping the baby's mouth with a cloth. "Are they not a wonder, lord? Would you like to hold him?"

"Oh no," he said, backing away. "I've no experience. I might harm it."

Hafren chuckled, plucking the babe from Agnes's shoulder to lay him in the bailiff's stiff arms. "You need a bit of practice, that's all!" The women exchanged an amused glance.

Godwin stared down at the baby, turning his back to the sun to shield his face. Eyelids fluttered, then opened, and two large gray eyes gazed up at his. A wonder, indeed, he thought, marveling at the tiny hands flexing and grasping air. A chubby foot kicked free of its swaddling.

"Aye, it's a miracle we are here together," Agnes said, tucking in the blanket, only to have a plump leg thrust it away again. "If it were not for the skills of the midwife, my babe would have no ma."

Hafren nodded, offering no false modesty. "I was sore bent on saving my Agnes," she said, giving the women a brief hug. "Too many mums and babes have I lost."

It was midmorning when Godwin was finally free of his shire. The day was fair and he made good time, meeting few travelers on the road. He reached Jedburgh Abbey an hour past noon. Inquiring at the gatehouse, he learned that Constance and his mother had arrived in the late afternoon on the previous day and had left at daybreak that morning.

After watering Saedraca and taking a quick meal from his pack, he set out again. Riding swiftly, it was not long before he spied another church tower among the distant treetops— Calkou Abbey. Good, he thought. With the few hours of daylight still left, he could get as far as Norham castle. There he would pass the night, for he knew its lord. On the following day he would overtake his party as it journeyed from Berwick to Dunbar.

The road straightened, creating an open stretch to the village of Calkou. He saw a lone rider racing toward him. It was William the Welshman. A cold dread gripped Godwin. His knight lurched to a stop when they met. "Lord, our party was ambushed north of Calkou. No one has been harmed, but Lady Constance was taken for ransom!"

"Where are the others?"

"At the abbey."

They raced to the village, William barking out details as they rode: five knights, no blazons, excellent mounts. They had knowledge of the party. The boy was their first choice, but the lady offered herself in his stead. They went north, she with the leader.

Godwin found his mother and the others huddled inside the gates of the abbey, curious villagers peering at them from the street. Gunnilda burst into tears when she saw her son, clinging to him like a babe. Eilaf stared miserably at his feet. When he saw his uncle, he said, "I should not have let them take Lady Constance." Hovering near was Bosa.

Godwin put a hand to his nephew's shoulder. "Lady Constance made the choice, and a noble act should never be denied or questioned." Eilaf said nothing and Godwin added, "But it can be repaid. When we have her back, you can show your thanks."

Godwin's knights were gathered in the street, awaiting his instructions. "Will we go after them?" William asked when Godwin joined his men.

"Oh yes," he said. His initial shock had been suppressed, and coldly now he put his mind to the task of getting Constance back. And never would he let her out of his sight again. His anger, too, he tried to stifle, but when he looked at his men, his eyes shone with it. He burst out, "Four bloody knights ambushed! By God's eyeballs, what were you doing?"

Burchard, Osbern, and Chadd dropped their eyes, but William gazed defiantly at his lord. "No highwaymen were these, but soldiers lying in wait! They had every advantage. If we had acted differently, one of your kin, or the lady, might have been harmed. We could not risk it. You would have acted the same, lord."

"Don't bloody tell me what I would have done, William!" People turned to stare as he strove to rein in his anger. William was right. He should have been there. Why hadn't he been?

He breathed deeply. "You are right, of course, William. Now let us concentrate on getting Lady Constance back. They've made no ransom demand?"

"Nay," William answered.

"I do not like this," Godwin said, passing a hand over his face. Abductions were not uncommon, especially in Border country, but ransom demands were almost always made up front, the silver promptly paid, the prisoner released. During wartime, it was a chillingly routine transaction. "I don't like it at all," he said again, reaching for Saedraca's reins.

"We'll not wait," he told his knights. "There is little risk her captors will know of our pursuit, for it's doubtful we'll catch up to them now. But we may be able to track them and find where she is being held."

William said, "They will assume we have come back to Calkou to wait. One of us ought to remain and deal with the ransom demand, should it be delivered here."

Godwin was reluctant. If they were forced to fight, he would need every man. Yet the plan formulating in his mind demanded stealth, for an open challenge might bring harm to Constance. "Burchard, you remain. Speak to the prior. We may need a loan from the abbey. Give them whatever they ask for. If you should have to retrieve Lady Constance, take Bosa, but not Eilaf. Take Duff and a canon as well and any sturdy men you can find in the village."

But Godwin did not think it likely a ransom demand would come to Calkou. Obviously, the abductors knew of their ties to Dunbar and the earl. Any demand would be sent there, where silver was plentiful.

Quickly, he went back inside the gates to tell the others his plan. "Stay until we return. Do not leave the abbey grounds." Moments later, he was leading his knights swiftly from the village.

William signaled when they approached the place where the party was ambushed. Godwin halted, going into the woods where the attackers had secreted themselves. But he found nothing, save flattened ferns and turned-up earth, as if they had waited a long while.

The trail was easy to pick up. In their wake, the abductors left a muddy swath of battered road. After many furlongs, Godwin saw a fork and raised his arm, telling his men to slow down. They went carefully to keep from spoiling the tracks. But it was obvious which way they had gone—along the main road.

They rode on until the evening light began to fail. It would not be possible to make Norham by nightfall, nor could Godwin chance missing any clues the road might yield. They watched for a clearing in the forest and made camp near the river. When the horses were watered and set to graze, they kindled a fire and broke out food from their packs.

It was an endless night for Godwin. He did not sleep, but sat apart from the others, going over every detail of the seizure. He roused his men before dawn.

"I am returning to the fork," he told them. "Ride on to Norham. If Lord Cowton is present, tell him what's happened. He'll surely offer help. Keep on the trail. They will be harder to track as you get near Berwick, but their passing will not have gone unnoticed. Question all you meet. If you discover their whereabouts, do nothing until I come."

"One of us should ride with you, lord," William said.

"Nay, it's only that I must be *sure* no one turned up that road. Likely none did, for her captors will want to position themselves near Dunbar."

"Then let one of us go," William insisted.

"No. Now ride. Leave word for me at Norham. I'll meet you at Berwick, or sooner." Then he was gone.

When he reached the fork, Godwin stopped to survey the tracks again. None went up the smaller branch. Still, he followed it. Nothing. The road looked like it had not been traveled in months. He was about to turn back when he saw hoof prints marking it farther ahead. When he examined them, he saw they came from the woods—no—from the verge. Someone had led a horse along the stony edge of the forest. Godwin slapped his head. What a fool! It was an old trick.

Quickly, he rode back to confirm his guess. Yes, here was where the horse was led from the main road. The prints all but disappeared, but now and then he picked out a partial imprint of a hoof, and a slight hollow left by a man's foot.

He urged Saedraca up the narrow tract. It was not a road he knew.

Up he climbed, spurring hard. The ground leveled and the woods thinned until Godwin was riding over a treeless moor. Up ahead, he saw signs of settlement, but they had the unmistakable look of abandonment. Far in the distance, he saw a horse approaching carrying two riders. As they drew closer, he saw that one was Constance.

TWENTY-ONE ✚

*Y*ou have done this?"

Fulk's gaze was innocent. "If you mean have I come to your rescue, then the answer is yes."

"Rescue?" Constance stared at him. "Then it was not you who captured me?"

His eyes widened. "Nay, I've come to free you." He walked toward her with arms outstretched, as if to fold her into an embrace.

She took a step backward, eyes narrowing. "It *was* you!"

He laughed, shaking his head. "I knew I would not fool you long, but I had hoped to garner at least *one* willing kiss from the ruse." He took another step. "Still, I will have it."

Constance moved to put the table between them. "But they wanted Eilaf. . . ."

"The boy? Yes, that is what you were meant to think." He stepped lightly around the obstacle, but Constance countered his move, keeping it between them. This was worse, far worse than anything she had imagined. "You will take me by force, then, since there is no other way? I knew you were unscrupulous, Fulk, but are you so depraved?"

He grinned. "Appeal not to my honor, love, for I have none. And do not pretend you find me loathsome, for I *know* differently." He took another step. "You realize how this game will end. Why not come willingly?" Breathing faster, his eyes roamed over her body. "Later, you can pretend I forced you."

She reached for the flask of wine, but his hand shot out over the table, catching her wrist before she could fling the vessel at him. Twisting her arm, he made it fall from her grasp. With his other hand, he swept aside the table. It tumbled away with a crash, landing upended. He pulled her roughly against him, locking her in an embrace. Constance writhed and twisted as he laughed softly into her hair. "But if you must resist, the experience will be equally enjoyable." She felt him tremble as he whispered, "When I am with another, it is your face I see, my love." He ran his hands along her back. Constance wrenched herself free, flying to other side of the room. But she knew it was hopeless. He was toying with her, the chase only heightening his desire.

"And once you have abused me? What then?"

"We will be married, of course. Did you ever doubt it?"

She gaped at him. "How will you manage it? By keeping me locked away?"

"If necessary." He started across the room. "You will not be the first prisoner bride." He took another step. "But words can come later."

She grabbed a candlestick, raising it over her head. "You think Godwin will accept this? My kin?"

Eyeing the brass stick, he hesitated, then sighed. "Perhaps I *should* lay things out plainly for you. You will be more willing after, seeing how pointless it is to resist. And I would rather have you willingly. You know that, don't you?"

She laughed harshly, still gripping the candlestick. "You have a strange way of showing it! But I'll never give myself to you, Fulk. You sicken me!"

"We shall see. But come, since you are so eager for speech, here's what I propose." He was all business now, the change dizzying. "On the one hand, you can resist. We shall be married anyway—plenty of false priests there are to bless our union. I will keep you locked away under guard. You will be moved from one stronghold to another, and you will *never* see your son. I will control his barony. All appeals from your kin will be rejected by the archbishop." He held up his hand. "And do not say Godwin will come to your rescue, for he shall be removed from office if he acts contrary to his lord's will. If he chooses force, he will be killed, for I have many more at my disposal than he."

"Many more in your pay, you mean."

He shrugged. "So? The other choice—far more pleasant—is to enter willingly into marriage. You shall dwell at Bordweal *with* your son, much as you have these past years. I will control the barony and will not trouble you overmuch." He gave her a lazy smile. "I have dreamed of getting you with child, Constance, seeing you grow large with my seed."

She was going to be sick, the nausea rising, filling her. "The archbishop does not control all law in the north," she said through clenched teeth. "Godwin and my kin will find justice in the royal courts."

"And what will they argue?" He spread his hands. "That I seized you, forcing marriage in order to control your son's inheritance? But what if *I* say highwaymen took you? Learning of your capture, I secured your release. I happened to be on errand to Perth. In your gratitude, you gave yourself to me, no great shame, for we had already contracted marriage—the archbishop will confirm this. Naturally, we wed, but after, you felt regret, through no fault of mine, and concocted your tale. No one of importance will believe you. The marriage will stand."

"You cannot be serious! Who would believe such lies?"

He laughed. "The court rolls are filled with them!

"But there will be witnesses, my family and friends, who will swear I never consented to marriage!"

"Yes, yes," he waved a hand. "And I will have my own. The summons and testimonies will fly. But justice is a slow business, and where shall you be in the meantime? With me, of course, carrying my babe, while your kin and Godwin futilely fight through the courts. In the end, I may pay a fine, but keep you I shall."

The candlestick dropped to the floor. What a fool she had been. There had never been a choice for her, except perhaps once, and she had thrown the opportunity away. Why had she been so selfish, so stubborn? "Why does the archbishop trouble himself over me?" she murmured. "Does he not have greater concerns?"

Fulk had gone over to right the table. He gave her a startled look, saying, "You think he has troubled over *you*? My dear, the archbishop's heard your name but once or twice and I dare say he dismissed it immediately."

"But . . . isn't he in league with you? You said he would reject the appeals, support your lies."

"My love, he does what I say when it comes to trivial matters. And he always supports those who are loyal to him."

"Even one who would capture and abuse a woman?"

"That is your story, not mine. He trusts the words of a vassal, not those of a woman."

"Are you sure? What if I could make him agree to *my* wishes? Would you abide his decision?"

Fulk cocked a brow, coming over to stand very close. She did not move, felt his breath on her forehead. Reaching down, he softly fingered a lock that had fallen to her shoulder. He asked, "What are you proposing?"

Constance still did not move or flinch. "A third choice— that we go before the archbishop."

Letting go her hair, he slowly moved his hand to her neck, running fingers lightly along her skin. "And what would you say to him?"

"That I do not wish to marry you, beg him to respect my wishes and my widowhood."

Fulk threw back his head and laughed. "Is that all?"

"It will be the truth. Can you do the same, or do you fear it?" He will not agree, Constance thought. Why should he?

His eyes glittered. "Fear the truth? Nay, I'm all for it, lady, when it serves me." The hand dropped to her arm as if he might pull her to him. But he only cocked his head to one side, considering. Then he slid his hand down to clasp hers. Constance knew then he would agree, for Fulk craved something more than a kidnapped wife.

"Very well, I'll do likewise," he said. "I'll say to my lord, here is the widow we spoke of. I desire marriage, but she is reluctant. I care deeply for the lady and will do my utmost to be a good husband. I will tend her son's inheritance and remain a faithful vassal to you, my lord. This I promise."

Constance gently tugged her hand free. "Then we are agreed? We go before the archbishop?"

"He *will* command you to marry me."

"If he commands it and can prove his power to enforce his will, I will freely give myself to you."

Fulk's mouth tightened. "Prove his power? There is no greater power in the north. Or do you hope to enlist the aid of your kin, or Earl Patric? That was not our agreement. We go alone before the archbishop and speak our truth, or not at all."

"That is all I ask."

He continued to eye her. "Women are strange creatures," he mused. Then he shrugged. "Very well, you shall have your audience with his eminence, and he *will* command you to marry me." Gently, he reached up to caress her cheek. "But must we give up this night?"

At dawn, the Saracen came for her. He led her back to the bailey where the rank grass was heavy with dew, the air chilly. The sun was too low in the sky to light the derelict courtyard, but Constance welcomed the cold as a long-held captive welcomes the first breath of free air. If Fulk were somewhere in the castle, there was no sign of his presence.

She did not bother to ask the Saracen where he was taking her as they left the fortress. They rode in silence, she keeping her gaze on the glorious sunrise, no longer afraid. "Tired, so tired," she murmured, closing her eyes. They flew open when the Saracen's sword came ringing from its scabbard. Ahead on the road she saw a horseman. Though still far off, she knew it was Godwin.

As they drew nearer, she saw that he, too, had his sword out. The men slowed their horses and approached warily. Godwin called to her, "Have you been harmed Constance?"

"Nay, I'm fine." She smiled faintly. "I'm very glad to see you."

"Release her now," Godwin commanded. The Saracen readily obliged, dismounting and backing away to wait as Constance climbed from the horse.

When she was safely by his side, Godwin said, "Go back the way you came."

The man sheathed his sword, smiled at Constance, and then leapt into the saddle. Godwin turned to study her, to see for himself that she was unscathed.

She had her arms around him before he could put away his sword. They remained this way for several moments. Finally, without removing his arms, he said over the top of her head, "Why were you released?"

Constance kept her arms around him. His back felt wonderful. He smelled wonderful, too, she thought, breathing deeply—like grass and leather. She reached a hand to finger a lock of his unruly hair. Every part of him was new.

Gently, he pulled her away. "Tell me what happened."

Constance sighed. "It was Fulk."

"Fulk!" His hands tightened on her arms.

"Yes. He plans to marry me with or without my consent."

"How did you escape?"

She laughed shakily. "By making a bargain with the devil."

"I'll kill him," Godwin said, as they rode slowly through the Tweed Valley toward Calkou Abbey. Constance had her arms tucked happily about his waist. She was discovering more of him, learning that his stomach was flat and lean, his hips narrow, like a boy's. "I'll run him through the moment

I lay eyes on him."

"That would be murder," she pointed out, studying his ears, or what she could see of them. He had a rather shaggy cut.

"It will be justice."

"Not in the eyes of the law *you* represent."

"This goes beyond law or justice. It is about protecting someone I love. If Fulk can take you once, he can take you again. I will not live with that fear, or with what he has done to you." His jaw clenched. She could see the muscles working, and hugged him, laying her cheek against his back. She had told him everything.

"Godwin, you cannot kill for revenge or to prevent something that *might* happen. As bailiff, you would imprison one who did. No one can be above the law."

He suddenly checked the horse, pulling sharply on the reins, saying, "I've been so blind . . . it is the same, yet different. Murder for revenge and to protect."

"Godwin?"

He urged Saedraca forward once more. "Yes?"

"I wouldn't want to begin that way—by killing."

He heaved a sigh. "I will challenge him to battle then."

"He would appoint a substitute."

"Yes, of course. Fulk's craven to the bone."

They went on in silence, Constance returning to the pleasures of discovery. There were so many things about him she had never properly observed, exquisite details.

"Still, he cannot get away with it!"

"I'll have my audience with the archbishop. That shall end Fulk's scheming."

"Are you sure, Constance?"

"Yes, he will have lost."

"And if Hereberht's plan fails?"

"It will not. And the archbishop will have no choice but to grant my wish. Can you be content with that Godwin?"

"No! I'll not be content until I bloody the man! May I beat him to within an inch of his life?"

Constance knew his rage would pass. She thought how different he was from Aidan. Her husband had been retiring, contemplative, brooding at times. With Godwin there would be no mysterious reveries, no withdrawals. There would be passion and laughter and abiding loyalty. It will be new, wonderfully new.

They fell into easy silence. Godwin knew he ought to be hastening to Calkou where his mother and the others waited, yet he wanted to prolong this time with Constance. He was still marveling at her return, that she was with him now, her arms around him in a way that was pleasantly surprising.

She was changed, he thought. She was as maddeningly rational as ever, but the reserve was gone. What had happened to her in that castle? He pushed away the anger that instantly reared up. She wanted to deal with Fulk herself, needed to, and within the law. He smiled ruefully. He was the bailiff, she the one abducted, yet Constance had more regard for the law than he when it came to dealing with Fulk. Even when she knew it favored some, the wealthy over the poor. But he knew what she would say to that. Law protected everyone. Without it, there would be chaos, with it, there was the potential for improvement, for creating better and fairer laws.

Godwin knew this, believed it, but he also understood that justice was unevenly dealt, that law was rooted in selfishness, created to protect the interests of his own class. One had only to study the great charter of liberties to see that the lauded freedoms largely concern the landed nobility—their inheritance rights and military dues, their rights to be judged by peers and offer counsel to the king. Was the charter granted to all in the realm? Nay, but Constance would say it was a start, a step, for if liberties can be extended to a few, it can be extended to all. Perhaps she was right.

"Godwin? Is what happened to me common?"

"Not common, but not rare either. One hears stories.

They usually involve heiresses and families whose wealth is great."

"Men can be despicable."

"I have also heard tales of women who have used such occasions to serve their own ends."

"What do you mean?"

"That a woman might arrange her own abduction."

"What? How absurd!"

Godwin smiled at her arch tone, his Constance. "I think it's rather ingenious. A woman chooses a man, but her family is against him—they have already picked out a son-in-law, say, or just do not like the chap. So she and her lover stage a capture. They marry and consummate the union."

"That is elopement," Constance pointed out.

"Yes, but the daughter can deny complicity. She cannot be disinherited. She can control her own fate."

They could see the abbey tower in the distance now. Godwin sighed as the tasks, unbidden, began to line up in his mind: send a messenger to fetch William and his knights, another to Dunbar, arrange tomorrow's journey home. . . . And whatever would he do about Gruffydd's death, now that he knew, without a doubt, that murder had been done?

"I can hardly wait to see Aldwin," Constance said.

"Tomorrow we shall."

She tightened her arms around him and, peering over his shoulder, saw a wide figure in the road just outside the village gates. It was Cynwyse, hands on hips, watching for their return. Constance thrust her arm up, waving enthusiastically, saying to Godwin, "She'll never let me out of her sight again, you know."

"That makes two of us."

TWENTY-TWO ⊙ ✠

This was not her first visit to York, but Constance still found the city daunting. Within its walls lay a warren of narrow, winding streets crowded with shops and homes and all manner of people. Towering above all was the vast Minster cathedral, drawing travelers and pilgrims from every corner of the land, gathering them to its feet like supplicants.

The Minster *was* York, for its presence everywhere dominated, a looming stone monument in a sea of timber. Even in the most twisted of streets, the most confined of alleyways, one could glance up and spy a tower, glimpse a clerestory window, or a square of thick polished stone.

Now, scaffolding covered the transepts, and workmen busily scaled up and down its walls like ants. Godwin had told her that portions of the cathedral were being rebuilt. The archbishop had bold designs for a wholly new church in the French style, one that would surpass even his archrival's in Canterbury.

Archbishop Walter de Gray kept Constance waiting for two full days before finally granting her an audience. Godwin and Cynwyse waited with her, though the cook often left the two alone as they kept company in a small courtyard adjacent to the Minster's guesthouses. Constance spoke little and became more agitated with each passing hour, growing more and more convinced that the archbishop would dismiss her claim. She was insignificant, a bothersome fly, and he would do as he pleased or as pleased his vassal. There was no hope of success. Then Godwin would take her hand and the doubts would recede, only to creep back as more hours went by.

A day they spent like this, from morning until evensong, then another. They had just taken up vigil on the third day when the summons came, delivered by a servant. Godwin accompanied Constance to the Chapter House where they found Fulk waiting in its dimly lit anteroom. He smiled and bowed slightly to each.

Godwin's face was rigidly set. He gave Fulk a contemptuous glance before turning to the servant. "Your lord is within?" When the servant nodded, he took Constance's hand. "I'll wait for you here."

Fulk opened the door and Constance cautiously stepped inside, immediately struck by the immensity of the room as her eyes traveled around, searching for its occupant. She found him seated on a dais, crouched under a mound of rich clothing. His face was lean and narrow with small black eyes that pierced her with a haughty gaze. Constance stopped well before the dais, sinking to her knees and lowering her eyes. "You find this Chapter House impressive, lady?" he asked, addressing her bowed head, scorn in his voice. "One day, when my church is completed, I shall turn my attention to this hovel, too. Now rise and come forward," he commanded, extending a bony white hand. "And be quick. I have much business to attend and no time for petty matters."

Constance stood, ignoring the hand offered by Fulk, and went to kiss the archbishop's ring. He noticed her slight at once and pounced. "Lady, I sense in you a willfulness that is unseemly. Perhaps it is unintended, nevertheless, it warrants correction. I shall instruct you, though great matters press me, for I am a man of the Church before all else." His eyes glinted as he said, "Women have but two models to emulate as they shape their lives. There is Eve on the one hand, the benevolent Virgin on the other. A woman can be unruly and wanton, or obedient and meek." He bent toward Constance. "The choice is hers, but instinct will beckon to evil, for mankind fell through a woman, and all women carry the taint." With mock encouragement, he added, "Still, she may overcome her nature, aspire to virtue by emulating Christ's Virgin mother, who questioned not the commands of her Master."

A ludicrous image sprang into Constance's mind: the Virgin Mary refusing the Angel Gabriel, shaking her finger at him, refusing to be the virgin bearer of Christ. "My lord archbishop," she said, "we are taught that mankind was brought to sin by a woman, but did not a woman also save us, by giving birth to Christ? I wonder, why is our nature likened to Eve and not Mary?"

The archbishop's eyes widened. "You dare to debate the teachings of the Church with me? Tread carefully! Be not obstinate! The wicked are punished, the virtuous honored."

Constance said no more, only lowered her eyes. His catechism complete, the archbishop went on briskly, though he continued to eye her with suspicion. "I cannot imagine what you hope to gain by this meeting, yet I will not refuse a vassal." He glanced at Fulk. "You owe him courtesy, not disdain. Now, what have you to say?"

She stood motionless, head lowered. Her eyes found a chip in the flagstone near the dais. Keeping her attention focused on this, she said, "That I deeply respect and honor my lord archbishop, but do not choose to marry his vassal, Fulk de Oilly."

"Obstinacy!" he thundered. "And why should your wishes concern me?"

"Because I have a writ from our king's regent, Lord Walter de Burgh, giving me license to remain a widow, should I choose. It also confirms my right to select my husband, if I desire marriage again, so long as my choice meets with the approval of my lord, the king of England, or his regent. I do not choose your man, lord archbishop."

Silence. "Show me this writ," the archbishop ordered.

She drew it from her sleeve. He snatched it up, unfolding the parchment to study it with elaborate care. He paid particular attention to the seal and signature at the bottom, and then favored Fulk with a brief smile. "I do admire the money-making schemes of our regent." His expression changed to a sneer when he turned back to Constance, "You paid a handsome price for this?"

"Yes."

More silence. Then he commanded, "Raise your eyes."

Constance obeyed. "Know your enemy, lady," he hissed. "You have bested my vassal and through him *me*, for I shall not challenge the regent over so trivial a matter." He tossed the writ at Constance and it fluttered to her feet. "But your victory has a price: my wrath. Return to your backwoods and pray you never come to my attention again, for I shan't forget this. My memory is as long as my reach, and my anger as enduring as my will! Now go!"

They left York the same day. Constance rode from the city in silence, victorious but savaged while Godwin and Cynwyse cast worried glances at her.

Godwin had not questioned Constance, knowing that in time she would tell him what had passed with the archbishop. The only hint he had of the meeting was revealed in the anteroom. Constance had fairly stormed from the Chapter House, Fulk on her heels. With the door firmly closed, he had said to her, "Constance, I never meant for it to go this way. He will not seek revenge, I'll make sure of it. You need not fear his wrath."

She turned on him then. "You are so certain, Fulk, as before, yet the meeting did not go as you planned. Now you have loosed a wolf on me, a creature beyond your control." She had gazed at him with pity in her eyes. "He is not your minion, you are his, and I find it a sad waste of a man."

Fulk made no reply, only went to rejoin his master.

Once they returned to their quarters, Godwin hastily assembled his knights, while Cynwyse packed belongings. They knew Constance was desperate to quit the city, though she said little and revealed nothing of what had passed, except to say he would not challenge her writ. Godwin feared he might be called by his lord to pay homage and give an accounting of the fair or the progress of Brother Elias. But a party of royal officials arrived and thankfully no summons came.

Now, though they were several leagues beyond the city, Constance was still withdrawn. "Lady, brighten up!" Cynwyse burst out, hastening her pony alongside her mistress. "Ye beat them! Ye should be merry!"

"Nay, it was Hereberht who beat them. I did nothing."

"Ach! How can ye utter such a thing? Did our steward face the archbishop? As mean as a wasp he is, but ye stood up to him!"

The road bore many travelers, mostly those headed to York from the north, and they passed several parties of pilgrims. William, Osbern, and Burchard remained alert and cautious, no doubt recalling the disastrous journey to Dunbar. Godwin rode quietly alongside Constance. He did not press her to speak, but hoped she might. Yet when he glanced over and saw slow tears spilling down her cheeks, he could stand it no longer. He pulled on his reins and brought the party to a halt. Dismounting, he went to stand beside her horse, and keeping his voice low said, "My love, don't cry! Walter de Gray is a cruel man, and his harsh tongue is legendary—I've been lashed with it on many occasions—but do not take his words to heart, whatever he may have said. He spoke out of frustration, for it is not often that a woman stands her ground before him!"

The knights moved discretely away, but Cynwyse urged her pony closer. "He's right, lady! Ye beat him at his own game. Now ye must put it behind ye and think about what's to come."

From her horse, Constance gazed down at Godwin's anxious face. "And the cost of my victory? I have drawn the anger of a great man. Will my son be made to suffer for it one day?"

"Never would I let that happen. I will always protect Aldwin—and you, Constance."

Cynwyse burst out, "Bless my bread, that's a proposal of marriage, lady!" She clapped her hands together, dropping the horse's reins.

Godwin gave the cook an exasperated glance. Looking back at Constance, he found her smiling. "Your words *do* sound like a proposal," she said. "Was that your intended meaning, Lord Godwin, or do we misunderstand?"

"It was a proposal, lady," Cynwyse answered for him. Then her horse, sensing no one at the reins, wandered to the verge to graze, taking the helpless Cynwyse with it.

"Yes," Godwin said, looking at Constance. "I desire marriage. Will you have me?"

"I must warn you I am penniless, for I have pledged everything to secure my freedom—dowry, possessions, even my marriage portion."

"Still the choice is yours. Will you have me?"

"I will take you, Godwin, for my husband."

He helped her down from the horse and clasped her hands. "I will take you, Constance, for my wife." He then pulled his signet ring from his finger and slipped it onto hers.

A group of pilgrims went by, traveling by foot. They stared curiously at the couple along the roadside, holding hands, then at the old woman flailing in her saddle, fighting to retrieve the horse's reins, and finally to an embarrassed knot of knights mounted on warhorses, rolling their eyes and grinning. One of the pilgrims nudged another saying, "Fancy that—a wedding party!"

TWENTY-THREE ✠

*T*he magic ship put in beneath a strong, well-built castle, controlled by a lord called Cador. He was fighting a war with a neighboring lord and had arisen early to dispatch his troops. Seeing the ship arrive, he went down to the harbor to board it, taking his vassals. They found a lady inside who possessed a fairylike beauty. Cador took her back to his castle, delighted with his prize, for he could tell the lady came from high lineage. He gave her a serving maid, and Nicolette was lavishly waited on and richly dressed. Yet through it all, she remained sad and preoccupied. Cador came often to speak with her, and admitted his love, pleading for hers. But she refused, showing him her belt: she would never love any man except the one who could open the strap without breaking it.

Cador was angry, saying, "There is another like you in this land, a knight who avoids taking a wife by means of a shirt, the tail of which is knotted. It cannot be untied except by using scissors or knife." Hearing this Nicolette nearly fainted. Cador took her in his arms and cut the laces of her tunic. He tried to open the belt but did not succeed. . . .

Constance looked up from her reading to survey the women gathered around. There was the midwife, her head bent intently over the shirt she was mending, her daughters tumbling nearby in the brown meadow. They still yearned to mimic the marvelous contortions of Matilda Makejoy. Aldwin was with them, sitting shirtless in the grass, thumb in mouth, mesmerized by the cartwheels and somersaults. Agnes was there too, her sewing in a heap beneath the bench as she nursed with dreamy wonder the babe folded in her arms. And Hilda was there, working a marvelous piece of embroidery, every stitch followed by a glance at her charge.

There was a new girl among them. Emma was a shy, serious girl who frowned in earnest concentration at her darning, though the stitches she labored to produce were slow and unlovely. Godwin had grown fond of the girl and her brother, suggesting they serve in their new household.

A breeze stirred the pages of her book, reminding Constance to return to the story. But still she gazed at her surroundings with sentimental fondness, keenly aware that all in her life was changing. She smiled at Cynwyse's soft snores, her head drooped over her bosom, a basket of shelling beans in her lap. The cook would miss the end of the tale, for Constance was almost finished. Timely, because in two days the household would be leaving for Dunbar. When she returned, it would be autumn. She would be married. Bordweal would have both a mistress and a master. Aldwin would have a father.

With a sigh, she went back to the tale.

Cador proclaimed a tournament against the lord he was fighting, sending for knights and enlisting them in his service. He asked Yves to come, as a special favor. He did, leading one hundred of his own mounted warriors. Cador received Yves as an honored guest in his stronghold. He then sent two knights to the serving girl, commanding her to bring the lady to the hall. She obeyed, lavishly dressing Nicolette, who went along, pale and wretched.

When Yves saw her, he could not believe his eyes. "Nay, it cannot be!" he thought. "It looks like the lady for whom my heart aches, but I know it cannot be she." He came forward and seated her next to him. It made Cador very angry to see them together. The lady asked if she could try to untie the knot in his shirt, and Yves summoned the chamberlain who was in charge of the garment. She undid it easily and the knight was thunderstruck. "Beloved sweet creature is that you? Tell me truly." He put his hands upon her hips and found the belt. "My beautiful one, it is you! I never thought I'd see you again! How did you come to be here?"

Nicolette told him her tale from beginning to end, how she was imprisoned in a tower by her husband, then of her escape and the discovery of the magic ship, and how Cador now kept her in his custody, guarding her in luxury.

Yves leaped up, crying, "My lords, here is the mistress I thought I had lost forever. Now I pray that Cador give her back to me out of kindness, and in return I will become his vassal, bringing one hundred knights to his service."

Cador answered, "My handsome friend, I am not so poor in warriors or harried by enemies that you can bargain with me for the lady. I found her and intend to keep her. I will defend the lady against you with all my might."

When Yves heard this, he gathered his knights and departed, defying Cador. They went to the castle of his enemy and pledged their service. The lord was overjoyed, sure the war was as good as over now with Yves and his followers on his side.

The next morning they assaulted Cador's castle, but it was very well made and they failed to take it. However, as the story of Yves and Nicolette spread, more and more came to join the siege and the stronghold was finally captured. Yves killed its lord and led his mistress away amid great rejoicing, all his pain now at an end.

Constance closed the book. The other women sighed with the contentment a happy ending always brings, but she found the story troubling, thinking how one man after another dictated the lady's fortunes. Still, she found love. . . .

"Lady," Agnes looked up from her suckling babe, her expression puzzled. "Was she not still married to the rich, old husband—the first bloke? What happened to him?"

Constance glanced down at the book, frowning. "I'm not certain, Agnes. The story does not say."

Hafren, without looking up from needle and thread, said, "The husband was dead. He was poisoned by the maid, so that the lady could escape and find her true love."

"Godwin, I must speak to you about the merchant." Supper was over, the tables cleared and folded away. Trunks were stacked in the hall in preparation for the coming journey. Godwin would soon be returning to Dilston Hall, but he showed no signs of departing as he held Aldwin in his lap. Her son was dozing, though he still clutched a piece of apple in his small fist. Cuthbert sat alert, eyes on the dangling morsel.

Leaning toward Godwin and keeping her voice low, Constance said again, "I think I know who murdered Master Gruffydd."

Godwin said, "It was the midwife."

"You know!"

"Not for certain, but . . . it fits."

"Hafren as much as admitted it to me earlier. She must have known about Asheferth all along. Who better to help Maegden arrange meetings with him?"

"Yes, and she must have been painfully aware of Gruffydd's treatment of her sister. She saw the merchant at the fair with the angelica and, being skilled with herbs, understood its purpose. She must have slipped away during the day to collect the water hemlock. Switching it with the angelica in the priory kitchen that evening would have posed little difficulty."

"Then she hoped it would be blamed on the leech—as an accident?"

"Yes, but to make sure, she went to his booth that night and added water hemlock to his stores. The moon was full, there would have been enough light. She stayed with her sister in town the night of the murder. It would not have been difficult to steal away, evade my guards, and break into the stall."

"Oh, Godwin, what will you do?"

He was silent a moment. "I am not certain that I'll do anything."

"But . . . she's a murderer."

"If she did kill Gruffydd, it was because he threatened Maegden's life. She was protecting her kin. Would you not do the same?"

"By taking a life?" she whispered. "Never, nor would you!"

"She could be hanged, her children left motherless."

"But one cannot take the life of another," Constance insisted. "It is a violation of our most sacred law."

"Folk are hanged every day. Our laws and customs demand a life for a life, and what is law, but us?"

"You know the difference very well, Godwin," Constance said harshly. "You are seeking ways to excuse her actions. Hafren should have sought justice through the law, not take it in her own hands."

The apple fell from Aldwin's hand and Cuthbert, patience rewarded, swiftly took it up. Godwin gathered the boy closer, saying, "You cannot find what is not there, Constance. A man can thrash his wife at will—no law says he mayn't. Was the midwife to wait until he beat Maegden to death before seeking justice?"

Constance was silent. Looking at her son resting peacefully within Godwin's arms, she knew she would do anything to protect their lives. Lowering her eyes, she studied the heavy ring upon her finger. Godwin's device was the oak leaf entwined with ivy: bravery tempered by fealty. She would let the matter go if that was his decision. It was not right, nor was it wrong, but perhaps it was the best they could do, all they could hope for.

In Sara Conway's first book, *Murder on Good Friday*, Lord Godwin has just accepted the post of bailiff of Hexham when the body of a young boy is found on the day after Easter. The wounds and markings on his body are shocking, and Godwin reckons that he was murdered on Good Friday. But why would someone kill a child? And why would his body be marked in imitation of the crucifixion of Christ?

An excerpt from *Murder on Good Friday* begins on the following page.

MURDER ON GOOD FRIDAY,

an excerpt ✠

PROLOGUE

It was the thirtieth day of March in the year 1220, the day
after Easter, when young Gwyn found the body. She came
upon it in the meadow just south of town, where she had
been sent by her mother to collect an herb needed for treating her ailing younger brother, Siward.

"Betony will be difficult to find so early in the season," her
mother had warned as Gwyn eagerly prepared for her outing,
bundling herself in a heavy woolen cloak and taking up her
gathering basket. "It will only be a tiny stalk growing among
the grasses."

Their stores of remedies and decoctions were low, for it
had been an unusually harsh winter, and most had been
consumed treating the many maladies that accompany the
wearying cold of that season. Nor it seemed was Winter yet
inclined to loosen his chilly grasp. As Gwyn made her way
into the nearby fields to begin her search, the bitter March
wind continued to blow, scudding and puffing over the landscape, bullying a pale sun, whose newly dawned rays did little to warm her as she stooped over the stunted grasses. She
hunkered down to scratch at the earth with a tiny finger, her
practiced eye roving over the ground.

Feeling suddenly daunted, she looked up and stared across the wide meadow. The early hour and biting cold made for a deserted pasture, with only gusts of wind for company.

Then she recalled Siward, sick and needful in his bed near the hearth, and was roused to mind her task. And to stave off the oppressive solitude, she decided to sing a song as she hunted—a rhyme to accompany her, one of many Gwyn had memorized to help in learning the healing properties of herbs. Her tiny child's voice was barely audible in the remote expanse, even in her own ears, as the words were cruelly snatched away by the wind:

> *Betony, betony*
> *O virtuous betony!*
> *Guards against evil*
> *In amulet form.*
> *Mends cuts and sores*
> *As a poultice worn.*
> *Headaches and coughs*
> *Will surely flee*
> *When virtuous betony*
> *Is sipped as a tea.*

She ended with a few skips, then pondered singing another—the hymn to horehound maybe? But she halted after the first verse, finding the songs were doing little to bolster failing spirits, her solitary voice only underscoring her aloneness. Time to get on with the task, she decided, knitting sandy-colored brows in earnest concentration. Once the betony was found, she could leave this dreary place and return to the warmth and comfort of home. Eyes carefully trained to the ground, she took one slow step after another, like a fox stalking prey, ready to pounce the moment her quarry was within plucking distance.

She halted in frustration. Not a single shoot located, and if she didn't return home soon her mother would begin to worry. She tried to recall the place where last summer they had discovered a large patch of the herb. Gazing across the expanse of stubbled green, she remembered that it had been somewhere near the eastern edge of the meadow, where grasses meet woodland, that threshold-like place where the illuminated world gives way to the shrouded and secretive realm of the forest.

That day, as her mother had gathered for her stores, Gwyn had rested in the coolness of the sun-dappled shade, while peering into the shadowy woodland realm. Children were cautioned by their elders to keep away from the forest. Young ones might become lost in the vast woods, starving to death before they could be found. Thieves and vagabonds were also known to hide there, and little ones would be easy game for desperate outcasts. The children knew, however, that much worse than mere mortals dwelled in the forest. The Wild Huntsman stalked its murky depths, accompanied by his troop of unbaptized souls, and children were especially longed-for prey.

Studying the gloom, she had sensed a quiet watchfulness inside the forest, a presence that made her at once uneasy and curious. She had wandered in a ways, reassured and emboldened by the presence of her mother, daring herself to go farther. And the deeper into the woods she had gone, the quieter and more guarded the forest seemed to become. Yes, she had thought, it would be easy to become lost once the comforting edge of the meadow was out of sight.

Then her mother had called, and it was with relief that she had turned from the forest's stifling interior. But once her back was turned to the dimness, she was seized by a desire to run, headlong, as though the unseen presence were now chasing her, bent on capturing the impertinent child who had dared enter its domain. It bore down on her, and Gwyn had sprinted for her life, stumbling and lurching through the leafy deadness of the forest floor. She was almost within its grasp, feeling moist, hot breath on her back, hearing the whoosh of demonic arms beating air as they strained to reach her.

Finally, she had broken free of the woods, springing forth into the safe warmth and blinding brightness of the summer sun.

Now the memory added to Gwyn's anxiety, and she decided to keep looking for the betony in the open meadow. She didn't want to go near the forest. She resumed her methodical, step-by-step search, but did not find the elusive herb. Instead, Gwyn found Alfred, the brewer's son, one of her playmates.

She stared down at him as he lay on his back, arms splayed. He was lying amongst the tall brown stalks of a long-dead plant, and she recoiled at the sight of his piteous body; for it was immediately apparent by the frozen look of terror on Alfred's colorless face, by the weird stiffness of his limbs, that he was dead. Gwyn jammed a fist to her mouth, dropping her empty basket. She shook her head violently, rejecting the sight. Then, with nightmare-like slowness, she began to back away, anxiously scanning the meadow around her, eyes pulled to the dark line of trees in the distance. Had the Wild Huntsman of the forest killed Alfred? Could he still be near, stalking her now? In an instant she was running, making for home and hearth with lightning speed, driven by the certainty that once again she was running for her life, knowing that poor Alfred had not been able to run fast enough.

⊙ΠE

Lord Godwin sat at a large plank table occupying one corner of Hexham's great Moot Hall, an imposing stone structure situated on the east side of the Market Square, directly opposite the priory church dedicated to St. Andrew. Erected long ago to serve the needs of the bailiff, keeper of justice on behalf of the archbishop of York, the Moot Hall uncompromisingly dominated the marketplace, a potent reminder of the shire's powerful overlord, Archbishop Walter de Grey.

With arms propped on the table, dark head held in his hands, Godwin sat staring at a large pile of documents—writs delivered last week by an agent of the archbishop. He could ignore the directives from his lord no longer, and with weary fortitude took one up and cracked open its seal to scan the contents. But his eyes quickly strayed from the tight cursive script, reading no more than the formula salutation. Loath to go further, he knew he would find the order disagreeable.

He had held the office of bailiff for eight months now, assuming it upon his return from crusade, still finding certain of its duties difficult to bear. At times he questioned his impulsive bid for the post and was well aware that others, too, shirefolk and kin, puzzled over his motives. Why does the lord of Dilston Hall, nephew of Earl Patric, crave to be bailiff? A sheriff, he is, collecting fines and fees for that greedy man, the archbishop. Why does he break up tavern brawls and run down petty thieves and knaves when he could be at tournament, winning honor, or serving the earl? Silver aplenty he has, so why take the job?

It was true that many men of Godwin's stature would contemptuously reject the office. Before the crusade to Damietta, Godwin himself would not have considered becoming a bailiff. What skills had he in justice? His training was in war. At thirty-five years old, his rugged looks and weathered features attested to a life spent out-of-doors, in the saddle hunting, tourneying, and campaigning. Middling in height and compact in form, his sturdy yet supple body bore witness to wide experience in the physical labors of armed conflict, while a calm composure and easy assurance marked him as a natural leader.

Yet fourteen months in the East with the endless battles and deaths of so many valiant men, Christian and infidel alike, had left him reconsidering his lifelong aims and pursuits. Rendering justice had seemed a noble course to follow. Besides, these were quiet times. The civil war between King John and the barons was well over, Magna Carta won: the king's will was now subject to predictable and customary law. A boy, John's thirteen-year-old son Henry, sat on England's throne, his regents busily putting matters in order at home; campaigns abroad to recapture lands lost to the French king would be a long time in coming. And here in the north, the Marches, too, were quiet, a wary peace in force between England and Scotland. Yes, a time for new beginnings, for tending to household and tenants and lands under the plow.

With a heavy sigh, Godwin forced his attention back to the writ.

All at once, he was on his feet, chair careening across the floor behind him. "By God's eyeballs, I won't do it!" he roared, banging a fist on the table. The pile of letters jumped and toppled. His eleven-year-old nephew, Eilaf, who had been dozing near the hearth where he tended its fire, jumped as well. Godwin looked his way and gave the boy a weak smile, as if to apologize, but Eilaf thought it a grimace and went to fetch more wood. It seemed that letters from the archbishop never heralded good tidings; rather, they ushered in periods of perturbed gloom for Godwin, times when Eilaf found it best to stay clear of the bailiff; for his uncle's frequent disgust with directives from his overlord sometimes compelled him to give rein to an already quick temper, making him unpleasant company.

Godwin retrieved his chair and banged it back into place. Regretting his outburst, he watched Eilaf sidle out the door. The archbishop, or rather his agents, for such a noble man of the Church would never soil himself directly with such base matters, had just ordered the bailiff to seize the goods and property of a tenant who had failed to pay a debt. The man was Guthlaf, one of the town's fullers. Godwin knew that a recent spell of bad luck had left him unable to pay most of his debts, forcing him to pawn virtually everything he owned. All that did not pertain to his craft of scouring and cleansing newly woven cloth, that is. Godwin knew he could never bring himself to seize the man's remaining possessions, for these were his only means to recovery. He would simply have to stall in responding to the writ, though he was acutely aware that another would soon be fired off demanding to know what action the bailiff had taken.

Experience told Godwin that it was no use trying to reason with the archbishop's agents, explaining, as he once had tried, that by leaving a man his trade, the debt would eventually be paid, impoverishment averted.

"Such charity," they had sternly reminded, "would make the archbishop a pauper himself. He cannot save every Christian from disaster. Besides, the income from his liberties and franchises benefits the entire English Church. Matters must be viewed from this larger perspective, Lord Godwin. As a man of the archbishop, your duty is to put his interests first."

Godwin had come to understand his duties very well indeed. As a liberty of the archbishop, all pleas of the crown and common law matters were dealt with by his court and its chief executive officer in Hexham, the bailiff. Godwin had been drawn to the prospect of dispensing justice, righting wrongs. But more often he was required to perform tasks that were quite unjust, to his way of thinking, as in the seizure of goods and chattels and the imposition of onerous fines. He hadn't, of course, expected exceptional Christian munificence on the part of his new lord simply because he occupied a Church office. Godwin was well aware that high Church offices were conferred by the king, these days his regents, as a reward to secular men for exceptional services rendered. Piety was not a consideration.

Yet he had been unprepared for the ruthlessness and ceaseless dedication with which the archbishop and his court exercised authority over the liberty of Hexhamshire. An agonizingly close account of all rents and taxes due was kept, as were accounts of all pleas and petitions to the archbishop's court. The business of justice, Godwin had quickly discovered, was a lucrative one as countless small filing fees and amercements added up to considerable amounts of silver. Never a single shilling due escaped the archiepiscopal court's attention.

He sat down again, determined to dispense with the unpleasant business of the writs as quickly as possible. The directive concerning Guthlaf was placed at the bottom of the pile. He would delay action against the fuller for as long as possible, until he could help the man find a way out of his predicament. No sooner had Godwin picked up the next writ, though, than the big oak door of the Moot Hall was thrown open. Fara, Hexham's herbalist and healer, came blowing in like an unexpected gale.

She stood for a moment just inside the doorway, breathless, one hand clutching long woolen skirts hiked to her shins. Frantically she looked about, startled brown eyes wide and searching, then relieved when they lighted on Godwin.

Quickly he came from behind his desk to meet her, concerned. Never had he seen the healer, always calm and composed, so distraught.

Youthful looks belied Fara's twenty-seven years, although a serene, almost grave, nature called to mind a wise and learned elder. Well schooled and practiced in the ways of healing, she had mastered the art under her mother's tutelage, just as Gwyn now learned from Fara.

"My Lord, I have dreadful news!" she cried, hurrying forward. "Gwyn has discovered a body in the town pasture! She says it is Alfred, the brewer's boy!"

Godwin listened as she repeated the tale of grisly discovery. Then he called to Eilaf, who was standing nearby, tightly clutching the pile of wood he held in his arms. Alfred was his playmate, Godwin realized, feeling a sharp pang of regret for his nephew.

His sister's son, Eilaf served Godwin just as Godwin and his cousin Aidan had served their uncle, Earl Patric. For most boys of good birth and lineage, at age eleven or thereabouts, entered the service of an honored kinsman to learn the ways of knighthood and lordship, of battle and command. Godwin remembered well his first year in service, his first time away from mother and sister. Still a child, but yearning for manhood, he had been at once excited and terrified, adventure hungry and homesick. Eilaf, Godwin thought, gazing at his lanky, fair-haired nephew, all angles and sharply protruding bones, was like that long-ago youth, fragile one moment, the next chafing for responsibility while still delighting in childish pranks and horseplay.

As gently as he could, Godwin said, "Eilaf, run quickly to the priory and fetch Bosa. He's delivering letters from the archbishop to Prior Morel. Then find Wulfstan. He should be just finishing his rounds and likely resting up at Watt's tavern. Send them both to the south fields."

Turning back to Fara, he said, "Will you accompany me? It may be that Gwyn is mistaken, that Alfred still lives and needs your skills."

"Of course, my lord." But Fara knew it was unlikely that her daughter was mistaken. Everyone recognized death, for it lived among them, a part of life, and the young were seldom sheltered from its indiscriminate harvest of souls.

While Eilaf dashed off in the direction of the priory, Fara and Godwin hastened through the quiet streets toward the common fields, attracting little attention, for it was still early, only an hour or so past Prime. Quickly they followed the tiny imprints of Gwyn's feet in the frosty grass to the body, but when they saw Alfred, they both knew that he was dead. Fara kneeled to gently press fingers against his small neck, noting that the flesh beneath her touch was cold.

"He's been dead for some time," she said, slowly drawing back her hand.

Godwin stood rooted, staring down at Alfred. He had fully expected to find the boy alive, sick perhaps, or even feigning to frighten poor Gwyn. He had not been prepared for this.

As a soldier, he had seen countless men die in a myriad of battles, had seen the innocent killed because they had the misfortune of being in the path of war's destruction. Yet he had never seen a child he knew brutally murdered. Choked to death it appeared, for Alfred's face wore the unmistakable expression of strangulation. Godwin felt a sick revulsion wash over him as Fara looked up, her eyes pleading the bailiff for an explanation.

With great effort, he suppressed his shock and tried to push away his last memory of Alfred—a carefree child capering about the streets of Hexham, reveling in the festivities that accompany Holy Week. Godwin kneeled down, like Fara, to feel the cold stiffness of the body and study the boy again. Calling on his long experience in battle, he guessed that Alfred had died two or perhaps three days ago, though the unusual cold made estimating difficult. Strange, he thought, that his folks have not come forward to report him missing. There was an explanation he was sure, for he could never imagine the couple capable of foul play.

Godwin knew that they adored their son, and his stomach clenched at the prospect of delivering the news of Alfred's death.

His deputies, Wulfstan and Bosa, came running over, both short of breath. They stopped abruptly to stare down at the boy. Godwin looked up, suddenly anxious for Bosa. Studying his deputy's large, gentle face, he saw an initial look of horror give way to grieving pain as recognition of Alfred slowly registered. Godwin regretted summoning him and cursed his lack of foresight.

He did his best to shield Bosa from life's darker elements and was reminded once again that he had been an unlikely candidate to serve as vassal in Godwin's knightly retinue. His father, however, had been determined to see him enter the ranks, as was his right by hereditary tenure. And to Godwin's pleasure, taking Bosa into service had improved the relationship between father and son; the former was less embarrassed by his hulking boy, huge and strong as an ox, yet gentle as a lamb and as easily startled. Bosa himself, it seemed, had transferred all filial devotion to his new lord, likely grateful to be relieved of an overbearing father.

Yet Godwin had worried about the rough-and-tumble competitiveness of knightly conduct and its effects on Bosa. Thus, he had given his "ward" the additional rank of deputy with a mind toward keeping a closer watch on him, limiting his contact with the boon companionship of Godwin's other knights, good men all, but aggressive and prone to vigorous rivalries.

As a deputy, Bosa's duties were tame in nature, for in the quiet town of Hexham violent crime was rare; infrequent drunken brawls outside the alehouse and heated exchanges between customer and vendor on Market Day were more typical expressions of hostile behavior. But even in these simple cases, Bosa was useless and likely to be the victim of any abuse. He got on best with the town's children and could often be seen striding through the streets with several hanging from his huge limbs. He and Eilaf had become fast friends. Once, Godwin had asked how, given the choice, he would choose to spend his life, fully expecting him to admit a desire for the cloister. Bosa had only looked confused, then alarmed, as if Godwin were hinting he should consider another occupation.

Now he looked on the verge of tears, and Godwin stood up quickly, saying, "Bosa, go back to the priory and fetch a litter—discreetly. I don't want half the town out here trampling the fields and nosing around. Tell the canons we'll soon be arriving with a body that needs tending for burial."

Bosa nodded slowly, then turned and lumbered back across the field. The three remaining stood gazing sadly at Alfred, slowly crossing themselves, one after another, in a succession of genuflections. Godwin tried to memorize every detail of the body and its surroundings. As bailiff, he had had little experience with murder. There had only been two in the past eight months, both carried out by bandits who had waylaid wealthy merchants traveling the southern route to Hexham. Motive and means were immediately apparent: to acquire silver by means of a crossbow, in one instance, with bare hands in the other. Neither case had been difficult to solve, and both criminals were apprehended after a relentless search of the shire's forests. Public hangings in the Market Square had shortly followed.

But this, the murder of a townsman's child, was altogether different. Who could do this, his mind kept asking. Why? Carefully he studied Alfred for answers, noting that he wore no outer gear to protect against the bitter cold, no cotte or cloak. It was impossible to say, Godwin realized, whether he had been killed in the meadow, or somewhere else and placed here after.

Wulfstan, still staring in shocked disbelief, echoed Godwin's thoughts, asking, "Who could do this, lord?"

Godwin knelt once more, gently turning Alfred's head to examine his neck. "Look here," he said, pointing to an abrasion circling the child's throat. "I'd say he was strangled by a length of rope. And see his left side? There's a knife wound there, though it doesn't look as if the thrust was deadly. Perhaps it was put there after death—notice how little blood came forth?" Something else caught his eye as he moved on to examine Alfred's hands: they were pierced, as if heavy iron nails had been driven clean through. He heard a sharp hiss from Fara as she caught sight of the bizarre wounds.

"Murder," his deputy was saying slowly, warily, as if he had never uttered the word.

Godwin straightened, his face grim. Though it was not apparent, he, too, was shaken. There was something wholly disturbing about the ritualistic injuries marking Alfred. He said, "Let's look about the field carefully, Wulfstan. There may be clues to be found as to who is responsible for this wicked act."

Fara remained beside the body, shivering in the cold as the men hunted in the nearby grasses. But their search turned up nothing, and Bosa soon returned with the litter. Alfred, now wrapped in Godwin's cape, was solemnly raised between the men and carried from the meadow. In the tangle of crushed grasses and weeds where the body had lain, Fara noticed a little patch of newly sprouted betony, white-green and twisted in a futile effort to grow beneath the pressing weight. As she stooped to pick up Gwyn's basket, she plucked some of the fleshy stems, wondering what evil had befallen the boy. A bane so powerful, she reflected with a shudder, that even betony could not guard against it. She hurried to catch up to the litter.

Alfred was carried in slow procession to the priory church of St. Andrew. Across the Market Square they went, where more people were about now, opening shops and setting up stalls in preparation for the weekly market. Heads turned to stare at the small shrouded body, and a cluster of curious townsfolk soon gathered to trail the solemn bearers up Gate Street, along the priory's precinct wall to its gatehouse. The inquisitive were stopped there, though, for Brother Michael was instructed by Godwin to keep them at bay. The thwarted onlookers shouted questions to the bailiff as he, Fara, and the deputies passed through the gates with their burden into the courtyard beyond.

Several canons awaited, alerted by Bosa, and they hastily led the party to St. Etheldreda's Chapel in the north transept of the cathedral. Godwin instructed them to prepare Alfred for burial, keeping an eye open for any clues on the body he may have overlooked. "His parents will want to see him," he added. "Tend him well, brothers, that they might remember their son as he was."

Then he set out for the brewery, to tell poor Gamel and Ada that their only child was dead.

Praise for *Murder on Good Friday*

"*Murder on Good Friday* is Conway's first attempt at fiction, but with it she put the arrow in the bull's eye with her story; the setting and even the feel of history all ring true."

—*GulfCoast Newspapers*, Gulf Shores, AL

"If Conway intends to continue with more mysteries to be solved by this medieval detective, she's set the stage well to join novelists like Tony Hillerman and Faye Kellerman who entertain with a good whodunit while introducing outsiders to native American and orthodox Jewish cultures. Conway has found a theme that reminds us that some pressing current issues have been with the human race for a long, long time."

—*The News-Star*, Monroe, LA

"Whether you're a history buff or not, you'll find yourself engrossed in this story and its characters."

—*The Third Age*